The
Dinosau

Tessa Krailing

Illustrated by
Piers Sanford

PUFFIN BOOKS

PUFFIN BOOKS

Published by the Penguin Group
Penguin Books Ltd, 27 Wrights Lane, London W8 5TZ, England
Penguin Books USA Inc., 375 Hudson Street, New York, New York 10014, USA
Penguin Books Australia Ltd, Ringwood, Victoria, Australia
Penguin Books Canada Ltd, 10 Alcorn Avenue, Toronto, Ontario, Canada M4V 3B2
Penguin Books (NZ) Ltd, 182-190 Wairau Road, Auckland 10, New Zealand

Penguin Books Ltd, Registered Offices: Harmondsworth, Middlesex, England

First published by Hamish Hamilton 1994
Published in Puffin Books 1995
1 3 5 7 9 10 8 6 4 2

Text copyright © Tessa Krailing, 1994
Illustrations copyright © Piers Sanford, 1994
All rights reserved

The moral right of the author has been asserted

Filmset in Monotype Baskerville

Made and printed in Great Britain by Clays Ltd, St Ives plc

Contents

Chapter One

Breaking Eggs

In a hollow cave deep beneath the Mendip Hills something strange was happening.

High on a ledge lay an egg, about twenty centimetres in length, with a cracked and wrinkled shell. For millions of years it had lain untouched, unmoving, forgotten even by the creature who had put it there so carefully, out of harm's way. Out of the way of Tyrannosaurus Rex, that fearful monster who once stalked the earth, terrifying all who dared to cross his path.

But Tyrannosaurus Rex was long, long gone. Gone too was the creature who had lived in the cave until a few months ago, when she left in search of a better hiding-place. But the tiny reptile curled up inside the egg knew that it had been abandoned and, gathering all its feeble strength, began to chip away at the shell.

Gradually the jagged crack grew wider; until at last one skinny foot, with tiny claws like fingernails, forced its way through to wave about wildly in the air. But all this movement caused the egg to roll dangerously close to the edge; and when the creature inside made one last gigantic effort to break free it finally fell into the deep, dark waters below, where it broke into a dozen fragments, releasing its occupant into the swiftly-flowing underground river.

At first the creature floundered and almost sank; but then some long-forgotten instinct came to its rescue and it began to swim, swept along by the current through tunnel after tunnel, until at last it reached calmer waters. Here it clambered ashore to rest, panting, on a rock.

And then, like all new-born creatures, it began to feel very, very hungry . . .

Simon Peter Richard Ogden − known to his friends as Sprog − awoke with a start and sat up in bed, his heart pounding. A bad dream . . . something about drowning, a real nightmare!

It was very dark. And silent. No sound of breathing from the next bed, none of the other boys snoring, not even Paul Appleby, who always snored.

And then he realized that he wasn't in the dormitory at boarding school. Term was over. This was the first day of the holidays and yesterday he had travelled down to Somerset to stay with his great aunt Cissie Stokes. That's where he was now, in the spare bedroom of her cottage in the village of Silverton. And in three days' time it would be Christmas.

Sprog put his head in his hands and

groaned. Now he remembered! Everything had gone wrong, all his plans changed at the last moment. Yet only a month ago he had been on top of the world. 'Great news!' Mum had written from the Middle East, where Dad worked for an oil company. 'Your father has been offered a new job in the UK, which means we shall soon be home for good.'

Home for good! That meant he would be able to leave the boarding school where he had spent the last two years and go to a day school instead. It was three long months since he had spent the summer holiday with his family and he couldn't wait to see them again.

'We should be with you by Christmas, with luck,' Mum had finished her letter.

But luck, it seemed, was against them. An airport strike meant that Mum, Dad, Francis and Meg would not after all be home in time for Christmas. Instead he had been sent to stay with Aunt Cis again. Not that there was anything wrong with Aunt Cis. As great aunts go, she was pretty remarkable. But nothing made up for not spending Christmas with his family.

He swung his legs out of bed and padded over to the window. It was still dark outside.

No street lamps, no lighted windows yet in the other houses. Silverton was a straggling little village, lying in a wooded valley. It had only one general stores which was also a sub-post-office, a pub called 'The George and Dragon' and a church where Aunt Cis played the organ on Sundays.

Sprog sniffed the air. Was that bacon he could smell? Aunt Cis must be cooking breakfast. He dressed and went downstairs.

She was already seated at the kitchen table, wearing her usual brown corduroy trousers and a thick green sweater. 'Good morning!' she said in a surprised voice. 'I was going to let you sleep late as it's the first day of your holiday.'

'I had a bad dream. It woke me up.' He went over to the stove. 'Can I cook my own?'

'Help yourself.'

That was the best thing about Aunt Cis. She never fussed or tried to boss you about. Tall as a guardsman, with short grey hair and a hooked nose, she could appear quite frightening to some people. She had even frightened Sprog until he got to know her better.

He broke an egg into the pan – and as he did so had an odd sensation of something

half-remembered, something to do with last night's dream. Drowning . . . and breaking eggs. How peculiar.

A primrose-coloured cat came to rub against his leg. 'So-So remembers me,' he said, pleased. 'She says she's glad to see me again.'

Aunt Cis smiled. 'I'd forgotten about you and animals.'

She meant, of course, the curious gift Sprog had for talking to animals in thought language without having to say a word. He must have had it always, but didn't discover it until he came to stay with her last Easter. That's when it had led him into the biggest adventure of his life.

He carried his breakfast over to the table and sat down. Gosh, he was hungry! And he'd cooked it to perfection – bacon done to a crisp, fried egg firm and crinkly round the edges, mushrooms browned but not burnt. 'This is great!' he said, tucking in.

'I'm glad to see you've still got a good appetite.' Aunt Cis poured some orange-juice into a glass and pushed it across the table towards him. 'I was afraid you might be feeling fed up.'

'Just a bit,' he admitted. 'But I like it here.' He fed So-so his bacon rind under the table.

'Even so, it can't be much fun, having to come and spend Christmas with an old fogey like me.'

'You're not an old fogey,' he assured her.

'Some folk around here might disagree on that score,' she said in a dry tone. 'Still, we'll do our best to make things go with a swing.'

'We?' He looked up hopefully. 'Is Talker here?'

'Sadly, no. He took off into the blue about

a month ago and I haven't seen him since. But then you know what he's like.'

Sprog did indeed know. Talker Harris – so-called because talking was what he did best – was a travelling man by nature. Once he had been a truck-driver for the haulage firm owned by Aunt Cis's brother, but since he had grown too old for the job she let him live in the loft above the barn. In return he looked after her ancient car and did odd jobs for her. That is, when he was around. He had a habit of disappearing suddenly, without warning, and not coming back for weeks.

'That's a pity,' said Sprog. 'I was thinking I might go up to the caves this morning, but if Talker's not here I can't.'

'Why not?'

'Because you always say that I mustn't go exploring on my own. Last time I was here you made me take Talker with me.'

Aunt Cis smiled. 'And a fat lot of help he turned out to be!'

Sprog smiled as well, remembering how poor old Talker had spent most of the time with his hand over his eyes for fear of seeing what he thought was a dragon. But of course it hadn't been a dragon at all. It had been a dinosaur called Minerva.

Aunt Cis said, 'Won't it make you rather sad to visit the cave again, knowing that this time it'll be empty?'

'Yes, I expect it will,' Sprog admitted. 'But I want to go. I feel I *have* to, although I'm not sure why.'

Except that it had something to do with his dream. The dream that had woken him up.

'In that case you must go,' said Aunt Cis.

'On my own?' he asked, surprised that she should give in so easily.

'Certainly not.' She poured herself another cup of tea. 'In the absence of Talker you'll have to make do with me. As soon as it's properly light we'll make a start. Now finish your breakfast.'

Chapter Two

Gosh, I'm Hungry!

Dragon's Tooth Cave was exactly as Sprog remembered it – a high, dark cavern with stalactites hanging from the roof. It smelled of dampness, like wet moss; and from the distance came the eerie sound of dripping water. He shone the torch towards the far end of the cave. Yes, there was the pool where he had first seen Minerva. Her great head with its strange helmet-like crest had risen out of the water, giving him the fright of his life.

'Remember that first time I brought you here?' Aunt Cis spoke from close behind him, her voice echoing around the cave. 'When suddenly your tooth began to ache.'

Sprog grinned. 'And you wanted to take me to the dentist.'

'But of course it was really Minerva's tooth-ache you were feeling because you'd picked up her thoughts.'

'And instead we had to bring the dentist to her!'

They both chuckled at the memory. Because the dentist in question had been Mr Spruce, who lived in the village; and when afterwards he tried to tell people that he had extracted a dinosaur's tooth no one had believed him.

'Poor man,' said Aunt Cis. 'In fact he was rather clever. He even managed to identify Minerva as a corythosaurus.'

'That was the trouble,' said Sprog. 'If he hadn't recognized her and made all that fuss she could have gone on living here for ever.'

'Oh well, I expect she's happier where she is now.'

When they had realized Minerva was no longer safe in the cave they had transported her to Scotland to join her 'Auntie' who was another kind of dinosaur living in Loch Ness.

Sprog frowned. 'Do you remember what she said, just before she disappeared into the loch? Something about a ledge, and a crack. I often wonder what she meant.' Unexpectedly his stomach rumbled. 'Gosh, I'm hungry.'

'You can't be! You've only just had breakfast.'

'Yes, I know. But now I'm ravenous again.'

'Then we'd better go home and make you a sandwich.' Aunt Cis turned away to the cave entrance. 'Coming?'

'In a minute.'

Despite his hunger, Sprog felt strangely reluctant to leave. He shone the torch-beam over the pool, half-expecting to see that familiar crested head emerge from the dark, still water. The cave where Minerva had lived was not the one he stood in now, but another chamber so deep in the hillside that it could only be reached by experienced divers using special breathing equipment. One day, when he was old enough, he intended to become a caver himself and explore those mysterious underwater tunnels the divers called 'sumps'.

He turned away; but at that moment he heard an odd little sound, like claws scrabbling on rock. At once he shone the torch onto the floor of the cave, but there was nothing to be seen except a few scattered boulders. It must have been some small creature, like a mouse or a rat . . .

There it was again!

He gripped the torch and shone it in the direction of the noise. There! Did something move, a small dark shape on the very edge of the pool? It was difficult to tell: the shadows cast by the torchlight kept shifting about deceptively. Suddenly he felt scared, as if he were in terrible danger. And weak – so dreadfully weak his legs almost gave beneath him. His heart was beating like a drum.

'Oh, don't be so stupid!' he said aloud, his voice booming round the cave. What was he afraid of? A mouse – or even a rat – was far too small to do him any harm. For heaven's sake, if he could face a full-sized dinosaur . . .

'Sprog? Sprog, where are you?' Aunt Cis called from outside the cave.

'Coming.' He turned and fled from the cave, blinking as he emerged into the winter sunlight.

'Are you all right?' She looked at him curiously.

'Yes, fine.' He couldn't possibly tell her he had been scared by something no bigger than a rat.

They walked in single file down the narrow, winding path until they reached the outskirts of the village. Most of the houses in the High Street were about a hundred years old; and some, like Dolphin Cottage where Aunt Cis lived, dated back even further. But there was one square, modern house that stood out like a brand new book on a library shelf. As they approached it Sprog quickened his step, anxious to get past as quickly as possible.

'Hello, Sprog,' called a high voice.

Inwardly he groaned, and turned to see Charlotte, the youngest Spruce girl, hanging over the front gate and smiling at him widely.

'Hello, Charley,' he said.

'I lost my front tooth. It fell out yesterday.'

'Yes, I can see.'

'The tooth fairy came last night and put 5op under my pillow. Are you looking forward to Christmas? We're having a party on Friday. I'll ask Mummy if you can come.'

'I don't think —' he began; then stopped as Charley's older brother and sister appeared behind her. As usual they looked unbelievably tidy, with pink scrubbed faces and neatly-brushed fair hair.

'Charlotte!' Her brother's voice was stern. 'Come away from there.'

'But Jonathan, it's Sprog. Don't you remember him? He came to stay with his auntie last Easter and he —'

'I remember him all right,' Jonathan said grimly. 'Now do as I say and come indoors.'

'But I want to ask him to our party!'

'We've got too many people coming already.' Caroline came closer and seized Charley by the hand. She gave Sprog a chilly, insincere smile. 'Sorry.'

'That's all right,' he said pleasantly. 'I didn't want to come anyway.'

Suddenly she caught sight of Aunt Cis. 'Oh . . . hello, Miss Stokes. I didn't see you there.' Embarrassed, she turned her anger on her younger sister. 'Honestly, you're hopeless! Come indoors this minute. I'm going to tell

Mummy what a bad girl you've been.'

She pulled Charley away from the gate and dragged her, loudly protesting, up the path. Jonathan gave Sprog one final withering glare before following his sisters into the house.

'Well!' said Aunt Cis, as they continued on their way. 'They don't seem any friendlier than they did last Easter. Mind you, I'm not altogether surprised, after what happened.'

'Neither am I,' Sprog said with a grin. 'The only thing that surprises me is that Charley still believes in the Tooth Fairy, even though her father's a dentist.'

Aunt Cis laughed. 'Let's get home and make that sandwich.'

'I'm not hungry any more.'

She looked at him in astonishment. 'Five minutes ago you said you were ravenous.'

'Yes, I know. But now I'm not.' He added apologetically, 'I don't know why.'

She shrugged and unlatched the gate of Dolphin Cottage.

'He's back,' Jonathan informed his mother as soon as they got inside the house.

'Who's back?' enquired Mrs Spruce.

'That boy,' said Caroline. 'You know, Miss

Stokes's great-nephew, who came to stay with her last Easter.'

'His name's Sprog,' said Charley. 'And I like him.'

Mrs Spruce, tall and willowy, looked fearfully at her children. 'Not the boy who started all that nonsense about a dinosaur living up in the caves?'

Jonathan nodded. 'That's him. The one Dad said kidnapped him and made him take its tooth out.'

'Oh, dear!' She sank weakly into the nearest armchair. 'And just when he seemed to have forgotten about it. He hasn't mentioned it for weeks. I was hoping he'd made a complete recovery.' She turned to Charley. 'Please, you mustn't tell him. Not a word. And promise me, all of you, that you'll keep away from that boy. As long as your father doesn't know he's here everything may still be all right.'

Solemnly they promised; but Charley kept her fingers firmly crossed behind her back.

Chapter Three

Mama!

'Very odd,' Sprog muttered, staring out of the window.

'What is?' asked Aunt Cis.

'Er . . . this book I'm reading.' He held up the paperback he had brought with him from school. The picture on the cover showed a space traveller battling against an army of onion-headed aliens.

'Yes, it looks odd,' Aunt Cis agreed, bending over the tapestry kneeler she was working on for the church.

Sprog's gaze strayed back to the window. *Very* odd, he repeated; but silently this time. And he didn't mean the book. He had had the strangest feeling all morning, ever since they visited the cave. No, now he came to think about it he realized it had started before then, with the bad dream that had woken him up. A kind of restlessness, that made it impossible for him to sit still for longer than five minutes at a time.

He put the book aside and stood up.

'Going somewhere?' enquired Aunt Cis.

'Er . . . up to my room, I think.' But he hovered uncertainly, digging his hands into his pockets.

'It's a pity about the Spruces,' she remarked. 'If only they were friendlier Jonathan would make a good companion for you.'

'Ye-es,' he said doubtfully. He couldn't imagine himself ever becoming 'good companions' with Jonathan Spruce.

She put down her tapestry and looked at him with concern. 'This isn't much fun for you, is it? If you like, we could go into Bath this afternoon and look at the Christmas decorations.'

Sprog brightened at once. 'I could buy some presents. I've got a bit of money saved up.'

'Good idea. Then you can have them already wrapped up before your family arrives.'

After lunch Aunt Cis backed the ancient

Morris Oxford out of the barn and told Sprog to jump in.

'I didn't know you could drive,' he said, surprised.

'Of course I can drive. It's just that when Talker's around I let him do the driving because he enjoys it so much.' She reversed very fast out of the gate and into the road. It was a good thing there wasn't anything coming, Sprog thought.

A car journey with Aunt Cis turned out to be every bit as hair-raising as a car journey with Talker. She drove as though she owned

the road, weaving in and out of the Bath traffic with a fine disregard for pedestrians and other motorists, eventually beating an irate-looking man to the last space in the multi-storey car park. 'It's all right, I know him,' she told Sprog when he mentioned that the man was shaking his fist at her and she waved back cheerily, as if in acknowledgement.

Bath was full of people doing their last-minute Christmas shopping. Sprog bought a silky green scarf for Mum, a board game for Francis and a doll for Meg, who was only five. 'What about your father?' Aunt Cis asked when they stopped for tea in the Assembly Rooms.

'He's quite keen on birdwatching.' Sprog bit into a sugary Bath bun. 'I thought I might get him a book.'

'Right, we'd better do that next.'

He enjoyed browsing in Waterstones, especially when he strayed by accident into the section dealing with prehistoric life. Naturally, when he saw a picture of a corythosaurus on the cover of a large, brightly-illustrated book he couldn't resist looking inside. And once he had started reading he found it difficult to stop.

'How about this one?' Aunt Cis appeared beside him, holding a compact birdwatcher's guide. 'It's only just been published, so your father can't possibly have it already.'

'That looks great!' He took it from her and leafed through the pages. 'If I buy it, how much money will I have left?'

Aunt Cis counted up. 'About three pounds.'

The dinosaur book was £7.99. Regretfully he put it back on the stand and paid for Dad's birdwatcher's guide. Then, leaving

Aunt Cis still browsing, he slipped away and used the remaining money to buy a present for her – a pencil-and-pen set in a special gift pack.

On the journey home he was silent and preoccupied. Strangely, although he had only just eaten a Bath bun he felt hungry again; and he found himself thinking back to this morning, when he had been seized with violent hunger pangs in the cave for no reason at all. Rather like the time he had felt toothache and it had turned out to be not his tooth that was aching but Minerva's. Because he had picked up her thoughts and also her pain.

What if . . .?

'It's getting dark,' Aunt Cis remarked, peering through the windscreen. 'I'd better switch on the lights.'

Suddenly Sprog realized what had been niggling at him all day. *What if it was not his hunger he had felt, but someone else's?* Someone hiding in Dragon's Tooth Cave, as Minerva once hid. That scrabbling noise he had heard . . .

'I'll have to go back,' he said aloud.

'To Bath?' Aunt Cis sounded astonished. 'But I thought you'd done all your shopping?'

'Er . . . yes, I have.'

Of course he had meant 'go back to the cave', not Bath; but it would be hard to explain, even to Aunt Cis, why he felt such an overpowering need to return.

Realizing she was still looking at him oddly, he added, 'But I didn't get any cards.'

'You can do that tomorrow, in the village. The shop has quite a good selection.'

'Oh, right.'

They went on driving, Sprog still busily thinking. He wouldn't be able to go back to the cave tonight. It was nearly dark already. No, he would have to wait until tomorrow.

But who could he take with him? If only Talker was here . . .

It's a pity about the Spruces, Aunt Cis had said. *Jonathan would make a good companion for you.*

Supposing he tried again to be friendly with Jonathan? If there were two of them Aunt Cis would raise no objections to them going up to the caves. 'If one person gets into trouble then the other can go for help,' was what she always used to say.

By the time they reached Dolphin Cottage Sprog had made up his mind. Tomorrow morning he would go to the Spruces' house and ask Jonathan if he'd like to go exploring with him. No need to explain why. Just say he wanted to visit the caves . . .

The last rays of the setting sun slanted through the entrance of Dragon's Tooth Cave, making a golden pattern on the floor. Feebly the newly-hatched corythosaurus raised his crested head and blinked. He was too tired now to be hungry. His claws were sore from scrabbling over the rocks in search of food. He knew he needed food, although he did not know what it looked like or where to find it.

Something else he needed too – something huge and scaly and comforting – but he didn't seem able to find that either.

All day he had lain amidst the pebbles. Two tall creatures with loud booming voices had come to stand very close to him, bringing light on a stick. He had tried to make them see him, but they had stayed only a little while and then gone away.

Now the cave was empty again, except for the golden bars lying across the floor. Perhaps, if he crawled a little closer, he might find whatever it was he needed. With a gigantic effort he raised himself up on his short front legs and began to drag himself towards them. Such a long ... long ... way. And when at last he reached the spot where they were lying he found they had disappeared. Vanished, seemingly into thin air, leaving the cave frighteningly dark.

Cold and starving and scared, Minerva's son opened his mouth to utter his first, instinctive cry.

'*Mama*!'

Chapter Four

A Good Companion

'Mama!' cried the baby doll Sprog had bought yesterday for his sister. Hastily he turned it the right way up.

'Meg will love that,' said Aunt Cis.

'Yes, she will.' But Sprog frowned. For some reason he found the cry disturbing. He was glad now he hadn't been able to afford one of the more expensive dolls that shed real tears and even wet their nappies. A doll that cried 'Mama!' was bad enough. He put it back in its box on the kitchen table.

'Aren't you going to wrap it up?' asked Aunt Cis.

'I thought I'd go into the village first and choose some cards.'

'Fine. And while you're at the post office you can get me some stamps.' She picked up her handbag, a capacious affair made of sagging leather, and rummaged inside it for her purse. 'Twenty, please. Second-class.'

He took the money she held out to him and put it in his pocket. 'I thought I'd call into the Spruces' on the way to see if Jonathan wants to come out.'

She looked a little surprised, then nodded. 'Yes, why not give him a second chance? He can't get much fun out of life, being so disagreeable.'

Sprog went to the door. 'I may be gone some time.'

'Be as long as you like.' She gave him a shrewd look. 'I know I can trust you not to do anything stupid.'

'I won't,' he promised, with a clear conscience. Even if she thought him stupid to go back to the cave, at least he was obeying her order not to go alone.

All he had to do now was persuade Jonathan Spruce to be his 'good companion'.

He collected the torch and took the path across the field, thinking that if he approached the house from the back he'd be less likely to bump into one of the Spruce parents. With luck Mr Spruce would be away at his surgery in Bristol; but Mrs Spruce had made it quite clear in the past that she disapproved of Sprog strongly, and she would certainly not encourage a friendship between him and any of her children.

Halfway across the field he paused for a brief conversation with Samson, the old grey horse now enjoying an honourable retirement. 'Don't worry,' he said. 'You're quite safe. Minerva's miles away, right up in Scotland.' Samson admitted he was relieved to hear it: he had never forgotten his first terrifying sight of a huge prehistoric monster lumbering through his field.

Sprog peered over the gate into the Spruces' back garden. At first it seemed empty; but then he spotted Jonathan kicking a football around, looking bored. This, he decided, was a hopeful sign.

'Hello,' he said.

Jonathan straightened and looked around to see where the voice came from. When he spotted Sprog on the other side of the fence he glowered and said, 'Push off!'

Not a promising start. Sprog decided to ignore it. 'Would you like to come exploring with me?'

Jonathan stared at him. 'What?'

'Exploring,' Sprog repeated. 'Up to the caves.'

'Are you bonkers or something?'

'Probably,' he agreed, thinking he must be bonkers to imagine he could hold a normal, friendly conversation with Jonathan Spruce. 'But Aunt Cis won't let me go on my own, so I need someone to come with me.'

Jonathan moved closer to the fence. 'Listen. Last time you came here you dragged my father up to those caves and he's never been the same since. My mother hates you. I hate you. Caroline hates you –'

'Charley doesn't,' Sprog interrupted.

'She's only a kid. And don't call her Charley. Her name's Charlotte.' He put on a menacing scowl. 'Now clear off.'

'You don't want to come with me, then?'

'What do you think I am – an idiot?'

Sprog considered the question. 'No,' he said slowly. 'No, not an idiot. I'd say you were more of a wimp.'

Furious, Jonathan took a step nearer, bunching his fist. 'Get lost, Sproggo! And don't come back.'

'Wouldn't dream of it,' Sprog said obligingly.

He continued walking across the field, determined not to give Jonathan the satisfaction of knowing he had messed up his plans. Of course, he could always go up to the cave on his own . . .

But Aunt Cis trusted him. On the other hand, he felt more strongly than ever that he must go to the cave.

'Sprog! Wait for me!'

He turned around to see Charley Spruce stumbling across the field after him. She was dressed in jeans and a hooded jacket and her face was smeared with mud.

'I'll come,' she panted, when she caught him up.

He stared at her, not comprehending.

'I'll come with you to the caves,' she said. 'I heard what you said to Jonathan. I was playing hide-and-seek in the bushes by myself. Are you going to look for another dinosaur?'

'No, of course not!' He realized he had snapped at her, and was immediately ashamed. It wasn't her fault that her brother was such a pain. 'Sorry,' he went on in a kinder tone, 'but you can't possibly come with me. You're too young.'

'People always say that.' Her blue eyes filled with tears. 'Jonathan and Caroline say it all the time. But I'm not young really. I'm nearly the oldest in my class.'

Sprog thought quickly. As long as he had someone with him he would be obeying Aunt Cis's wishes – and if by some chance he did get into trouble, Charley could easily run down to the village with a message. She might even make a better companion than Jonathan, because she wouldn't ask so many questions.

'Well, okay,' he said. 'But you mustn't come into the cave. You'll have to wait outside. Do you understand?'

She nodded, her eyes glowing.

'Come on, then.'

She followed him across the field, half-running to keep up with the pace he set. As they climbed the steep hillside towards the area known as Tibor Rocks, where the caves were, she kept up a breathless, one-sided conversation.

'Mummy's ever so worried because you've come back. She thinks if Daddy sees you it'll remind him about the dinosaur . . . and then he'll get upset again and start talking about when he pulled its tooth out. She made us promise not to tell him. Did the dinosaur get 50p?'

This last remark stopped Sprog in his tracks. 'What?'

'From the Tooth Fairy.'

'Oh, I see.' He grinned. 'No, I don't believe she ever did. I expect the Tooth Fairy was too scared to come close.'

They arrived at the cave entrance. Sprog said firmly, 'This is where you have to wait for me. You can sit on that rock over there.'

Charley's mouth turned down at the corners. 'But I want to come inside.'

'You wouldn't like it. It's dark and you'd be scared.'

'No, I wouldn't. Anyway, you've got a torch.'

'But you're the look-out. I'm depending on you to keep watch, and if anyone comes you have to warn me.' He added persuasively, 'It's a very important job, Charley.'

She hesitated; then said, 'Oh, all right.'

He breathed a sigh of relief. 'If I'm not out in ten minutes give me a yell – and if I don't answer you'd better go for help. But don't worry, I'll be back long before then.'

'I haven't got a watch,' she said.

'You can have mine.' He took off his red-and-grey digital watch and handed it to her. 'Look, it's ten-twenty now. When the figures say ten-thirty that means the time's up.'

She strapped it on to her wrist and stared down at its face. 'Ten-thirty,' she muttered to herself. 'Ten-thirty time's up . . .'

Sprog switched on the torch and entered the cave.

41

Chapter Five

Only a Baby

Sprog shone the torch over the glistening cave walls and down to the floor. Nothing to be seen. Nothing to be heard except the faint drip-drip-drip of running water.

What did he expect to find?

'*Are you going to look for another dinosaur?*' Charley had asked; and he had snapped, '*Of course not!*'

But that was not strictly true. Secretly he couldn't help hoping that he might find another Minerva. Impossible, of course. Minerva was unique, the only corythosaurus still alive. At least, he hoped she was still alive, swimming happily in the waters of Loch Ness . . .

'*Mama!*'

He jumped. Meg's doll — here in the cave?

No, he must be imagining things. He hadn't really heard the cry, it was just a thought that had come into his mind.

A thought . . .

He stood still, hardly daring to breathe, and swung the torch again over the cave floor. He had not moved far from the entrance. Some natural light illumined the place where he was standing, throwing into sharp relief a small boulder close to his feet.

Or – was it a boulder?

He peered closer, shining the torch directly on to the object, which now appeared to be less rocky than scaly and certainly a very odd shape for a boulder. Greyish-green in colour, with legs and a tail, it looked more like a stone lizard. A very large lizard, though, about thirty-five centimetres long, with a mouth shaped like a duck's bill. And it had unusual legs for a lizard – two short ones in the front and two longer, more powerful ones at the back.

Sprog's heart began to pound in his chest. Was it . . . could it possibly be alive? It looked pretty dead. Its eyes were closed and it did not appear to be breathing. He knelt beside the creature and gingerly stretched out a hand.

Suddenly one small round eye stared up at him.

He snatched his hand away at once – and at the same moment the creature opened its mouth, revealing a row of small yellowish teeth, and made a feeble little sound, like the mewing of a cat.

Tired. Oh, so tired.

Sprog felt the tiredness inside his own body. A great weariness stole through his arms and legs, robbing him of all strength. He sank down on the ground beside the creature and saw the little round eye begin to close . . .

'No!' He sat up abruptly. 'Don't die. You mustn't die. Quick, try to stand up.'

Forgetting his own tiredness, he grasped the scaly creature and lifted it onto its feet. It struggled weakly, but he held on tight. 'It's all right,' he said reassuringly. 'I'm not going to hurt you. I want to help you, whoever you are.'

But even as he spoke he realized that he already knew who the creature was. He could recall his dream quite clearly now, the egg rolling off the ledge into the water; the shell breaking, and the long, long swim through seemingly endless tunnels. 'She tried to tell me,' he said to himself. 'Minerva tried to tell me before she disappeared into Loch Ness. That's what she meant by the ledge and the crack. She must have suddenly remembered –'

'Mama!' cried the creature.

'You're Minerva's egg!' Sprog stared at it in wonder. Now he looked at it properly he could see the resemblance, except that it had only the beginnings of a crest on its head, not a proper helmet like its mother. 'That's who you are. You're a baby corythosaurus!'

'Mama!' it cried again, plaintively.

'And you're *hungry*!' He sprang to his feet. 'Wait here. I'll be back.'

He raced out of the cave and began to tear up grass and ferns, any kind of vegetation he could lay his hands on that was growing close to the entrance. Corythosaurus were not carnivorous dinosaurs: they fed only on plant life. Poor little thing, it must be starving. No wonder he had felt those hunger pangs yesterday.

'Sprog? What are you doing?'

He jumped guiltily. He had forgotten Charley. She stood close beside him, holding out her wrist to show him his watch.

'It's not ten-thirty yet,' she told him sternly. 'Your time's not up.'

'I'm going back,' he said. 'It's just that I . . . I need some grass.'

'What for?'

'Er – food.'

'You like to eat *grass*?' She looked amazed.

'Not me.' He thought quickly. This situation could be dangerous. If Charley were to see Minerva's baby and tell her father it might lead to all sorts of trouble. Somehow he had to find a way of putting her off the scent. 'I found a lizard,' he told her. 'I think it's injured or something. Anyway, it needs food.'

'Oh, can I look?'

'No, you stay here and keep watch.' He turned back to the cave.

'But I want to see the lizard.' She followed him through the entrance and peered into the darkness. 'Is that it, lying on the floor?'

'Yes – but don't come any closer. You might frighten it.' He knelt down beside the creature and dangled the grass in front of its nose.

'What's it doing?' Charley asked.

'Nothing.'

'Why isn't it eating the grass?'

'I don't know.'

He pushed some fern fronds right up against the creature's lips. 'Eat!' he urged, in thought language. 'You must eat, otherwise you'll die.'

It stared up at him with sad, bewildered eyes.

'Milk!' he exclaimed. 'I expect that's what it needs. It's only a baby, too young to eat grass. Perhaps it needs some milk.'

'It doesn't look like a baby to me,' Charley remarked, edging a little nearer. 'It's enormous, more like a crocodile than a lizard.'

'Stay where you are!'

She jumped back hastily.

'Sorry,' muttered Sprog. He hadn't meant to startle her, but he couldn't risk her coming too close. If she were to describe in detail what she had seen to her father . . .

He made a swift decision. 'I'm going to take it down to Aunt Cis's,' he said. 'I'm sure she'll know what to do.'

He peeled off his jacket and wrapped it around the creature's body like a shawl, leaving only its strange, duck-billed head poking out. It struggled a little when he lifted it up, but then the warmth seemed to have a calming effect. Holding it carefully in his arms, he walked towards the mouth of the cave.

'Won't your auntie mind?' Charley asked, trying to get a better look at the creature's face. 'My mummy would be furious if I took a crocodile home. She won't even let me have a kitten!'

'Aunt Cis is different.' *Thank goodness*, he added silently.

He set off down the path, with Charley close on his heels, and again took the short cut across the fields. When they reached the gate leading into the Spruces' back garden he stopped and said, 'Goodbye, Charley. You'd better go indoors now or your mum will be wondering where you are.'

Charley's mouth drooped with disappointment. She opened the gate; then turned back to ask hopefully, 'Is it a secret? Do you want me to promise not to tell anyone?'

Sprog hesitated. If she was anything like his sister Meg she wouldn't be able to keep a secret: and as long as nobody guessed what they had really found there would be no danger. 'It might be best if you didn't mention the cave,' he said. 'But you can say we found a lizard, if you like.'

'I'll tell them we found a crocodile,' Charley muttered rebelliously as she closed the gate behind her.

Sprog hurried on, knowing he must get back to Dophin Cottage as soon as possible if he was to save the life of Minerva's baby.

Chapter Six

Finding a Name

Aunt Cis took the arrival of a newly-hatched corythosaurus with remarkable calm. She had learned by now that when Sprog came to stay anything could happen. But when he asked her for some milk she looked doubtful.

'Dinosaurs are reptiles,' she said, gazing down at the strange creature lying in a nest of blankets on the hearthrug. 'And reptiles don't drink milk.'

'Not even when they're babies?'

'No, I think only mammals do that.'

'I tried giving him some grass,' Sprog said, 'but he didn't seem interested.'

'Too indigestible, I expect. Why do you say "him"? How can you be sure it's a boy?'

'I don't know.' But Sprog had no doubt in his mind. 'He just is, I'm certain of it.'

Aunt Cis looked thoughtful. 'Wait, I've had an idea . . .' She left the room.

Sprog knelt beside the little dinosaur and gently stroked his head while So-So the cat, crouched on the arm of a chair, watched them both with blue unblinking eyes. 'He won't harm you,' Sprog assured her in thought language. 'Poor thing, he's too weak to harm a fly.'

Aunt Cis came back into the room, holding a Waterstones bag. 'This was meant to be your Christmas present,' she said, 'but I think in the circumstances you'd better have it early. Luckily I hadn't got around to wrapping it yet.'

Sprog opened the bag and took out the book on prehistoric life he had admired yesterday. 'Gosh, thanks!' he exclaimed. 'But how did you manage to buy it without me knowing?'

'I waited until you were in another part of the shop. You'd better look inside and see if it says anything useful about feeding baby dinosaurs.'

He scanned the contents and found a chapter headed 'Family Life'. The picture showed four young dinosaurs in a nest, clamouring for food. 'Once the babies had hatched from

the egg,' Sprog read aloud, 'for the first few weeks they were most likely fed in the nest by their mother, either pre-digested or partly digested vegetation.'

'Just as I thought,' said Aunt Cis. 'Pre-digested means it had already been chewed up by the mother. I wonder if some of my home-made vegetable soup would be the answer?'

'It might,' Sprog said. 'Especially if we mash up the chunky bits.'

'There's some in the pan. I'll go and fetch it.'

While she was gone he went on stroking

the creature's crested head, willing him to stay alive. 'Food's coming,' he told him. 'You won't have to wait much longer.'

But the small eyes gazing up at him were already becoming glazed, the scaly lids drooping lower and lower.

'Oh please, you mustn't die!' Sprog pleaded. He wanted so desperately for the little dinosaur still to be alive when his parents came home. Although they had never actually said they didn't believe his story about Minerva, he could tell from their faces they thought he had made it all up. Even Francis and Meg had looked sceptical. But now, if only they could see Minerva's son, they would *have* to believe him.

Aunt Cis came back into the room, carrying a bowl of soup and a spoon. 'I've mashed it up as best I could. It's quite cool, so you can feed it to him straight away.'

Sprog took the bowl from her and spooned up some of the mixture. 'Come on,' he urged. 'You'll like this. It's got peas in it, and carrots and celery – all sorts of good things.'

But the duck-billed mouth stayed tightly closed.

'You may have to force him to take the first spoonful,' said Aunt Cis.

Once, on television, he had seen a vet demonstrate how to make an animal open its mouth. Rather gingerly he pressed his thumb and forefinger on either side of the jaw – and to his surprise it worked! Quick as a flash he pushed in the spoon and tipped it up. The little dinosaur coughed and spluttered, swallowing some of the soup almost by mistake. Sprog scooped up another spoonful and tried again. This time it disappeared in one huge gulp.

'Well done!' said Aunt Cis. 'It should be easier now he's got the taste.'

'It's a bit like feeding a baby,' Sprog said, remembering how he had helped to feed Meg in her high-chair.

'Yes, it is,' Aunt Cis agreed. 'In fact, when we run out of soup we might try him on some baby food. Strictly vegetarian, of course.'

She sat down in the chair to watch the little creature guzzling soup as fast as Sprog could shovel it into his mouth. So-so jumped off the arm to sit on her lap.

'Have you decided what you're going to call him?' she asked.

'Not yet.' Sprog thought hard. 'Did Minerva – the original one, I mean, the Roman goddess – did she have any children?'

'I don't believe so. But if his crest grows into a proper helmet like hers you'll have to give him a warrior's name. One of the Greek heroes, perhaps. How about Achilles?'

'What did he do?'

'Fought in the Trojan war.'

'Did he wear a helmet?'

'Must have done, otherwise he'd never have survived.'

Now he came to think about it, Sprog vaguely remembered seeing a picture of Achilles on a history wall-chart, wearing full armour and carrying a spear.

'Then we'll call him Achilles.' With surprise he noticed the bowl was now empty. 'Gosh, he's finished!'

Achilles made a loud burping noise.

'Listen to that,' said Aunt Cis, looking quite sentimental. 'Just like a real baby. I expect he'll sleep now for a while.'

Sprog drew the blankets over Achilles until only his crested head was showing. 'It's a good thing I found him when I did. He'll be a lot better off with us than down in that cave. I hate to think how long he'd have –'

'Ssssh!' Suddenly Aunt Cis sat bolt upright in the chair. So-So too was looking alert.

'What's the matter?'

'I thought I heard a noise.'

At that moment the living-room door swung open and they both turned round to see Charlotte Spruce. 'Hello, Sprog,' she said, smiling her gap-toothed smile. 'I brought back your watch. You lent it to me when you went into the cave.' She held it out to him.

'Oh, thanks,' said Sprog, when he had recovered from the shock. He hadn't even noticed the watch was missing. 'But, how did you get in?'

'Through the back door. I came over the fields because it was quicker. Nobody was in the kitchen, but I heard you talking in here.' Her eyes widened as she saw So-So sitting on Aunt Cis's lap. 'Oh, what a sweet little cat! Can I stroke her?'

'If you like.' Aunt Cis exchanged a helpless look with Sprog.

'I adore cats. She has lovely fur, so soft and pretty. What's her name?'

'So-So,' said Sprog. 'She's a Siamese.'

'I wish I had a Siamese cat.' She caught sight of the bundle of blankets on the hearth-rug. 'Is that the crocodile?'

Sprog moved swiftly to block her view. 'You mustn't come any closer. He's asleep.'

'Oh, let me look. Just a peep.'

Sprog hesitated. Only Achilles' head showed above the blankets, and if she were allowed a glimpse of him that might keep her quiet. In any case it seemed unlikely she would connect this small creature with the much larger Minerva.

'All right,' he said reluctantly. 'As long as you don't wake him up.'

'I won't,' she promised, tiptoeing nearer. 'What a funny little face. He looks more like a duck than a crocodile.' She swung round, her eyes shining with triumph. 'Now I know what he is!'

Sprog's mouth went dry. 'What?' he asked hoarsely.

'He's a *duck*odile!'

Chapter Seven

Someone Else

'For a moment she had me scared,' Sprog confessed when Charley had gone. 'I thought she'd recognized Achilles as a corythosaurus. But a *duck*odile!' He laughed. 'That's just the sort of daft thing Meg or Francis would say.'

'In future we'd better lock the back door. We can't risk any more intruders taking us by surprise.' Aunt Cis looked worried. 'If news gets out there was a baby dinosaur in that cave it'll be just as bad as when they heard about Minerva. News reporters, photographers . . . all sorts of people will come flocking round.'

'That's why I told Charley he was a lizard. Still, as long as she goes around saying we found a crocodile – or rather, a duckodile! – nobody will believe her.'

'We must hope so.' Aunt Cis got to her feet. 'I'd better go up to the shop and buy some baby food. Then we can feed Achilles as soon as he wakes up again. By the way, did you get those stamps?'

'Sorry, they went right out of my head.' Sprog took the money out of his pocket and gave it back to her. 'I didn't get the cards either.'

'I'll buy a couple of packets while I'm in the village,' she said. 'You'll be far too busy from now on to worry about Christmas shopping.'

'Yes, I will,' Sprog agreed, looking down at the sleeping Achilles.

'And when I come back we must decide what's to be done about Achilles' future.'

She picked up her leather handbag and went into the hall to put on her outdoor coat. When Sprog heard the front door slam behind her he sat in the armchair next to So-So, absentmindedly stroking the cat's soft fur.

What's to be done about Achilles' future . . .

He stared down at the sleeping dinosaur. Charley had been right in a way: Achilles did look a bit like Donald Duck with those little eyes, now tightly shut, and that pale yellow bill. The rest of him was greyish-green in colour and scaly, like Minerva.

But there was one important difference between him and his mother. Achilles was small. Portable. Much easier to hide. He could be kept in a secret place and no one need ever find out about him. In other words, he was pet-sized.

Sprog had hated saying goodbye to Minerva. He often thought about that moment when he had stood on the banks of Loch Ness, watching her sink beneath the waves. And she had hated leaving him, he was sure of that, even though she had gone to join her Auntie. But with Minerva there had been no choice: she couldn't possibly be kept as a pet. She was just too big.

But Achilles wasn't. Of course he'd grow bigger in time, but not for years and years. And in the meantime . . .

Sprog felt a shiver of excitement run down his spine. In the meantime he had a baby dinosaur to look after. Maybe this wasn't going to be such a bad Christmas after all!

Mr Spruce, tired of drilling holes in his patients' teeth, decided to knock off early and go home. After all, it was nearly Christmas,

and most people had stopped work altogether. As he drove through Silverton High
Street he saw Miss Cissie Stokes come out of
the village shop with a bulging leather bag,
and as usual the sight of her made him
thoughtful and a little depressed.

He found his family seated around the
breakfast bar in the kitchen, eating pizza.

'Christopher!' exclaimed his wife. 'What
on earth are you doing home at this hour?
Are you feeling ill?'

'No, I'm fine,' snapped Mr Spruce. Over the last two days she had shown unusual concern for his health, which he found annoying. He helped himself to a slice of pizza and hoisted his rather large bottom on to the stool next to Jonathan. 'By the way, I saw Miss Stokes just now as I drove through the village. I wonder if she's heard from him.'

They all stopped eating to stare at him. 'From – him?' repeated Mrs Spruce, pressing a nervous hand to her throat.

'That great-nephew of hers, the one who came to stay with her last Easter. I thought she might have heard from him as it's Christmas.'

He glanced around the table at their faces. His wife's had gone pale, Jonathan's was turning pink, Caroline's wore an anxious expression, and Charlotte's – well, Charlotte's looked as if she might go off bang at any minute.

'What's the matter?' he demanded. 'Have I said something I shouldn't?'

'Of course not, dear,' Mrs Spruce hastened to assure him. 'It's just that we – we thought you'd forgotten about – about –'

'About the time I saw a dinosaur,' he interrupted. A nerve began to twitch in his temple.

'No, I haven't forgotten. It's not the sort of thing one does forget in a hurry. Because I did see a dinosaur, no matter how hard everyone tries to convince me I didn't. And that young man, the one who calls himself Sprog, knows I did!'

You could have heard a pin drop on the kitchen floor. Everyone sat paralysed, staring at Mr Spruce.

His wife was the first to recover. 'Well dear, I'm sure you've had a busy day. We've been very busy – haven't we, children? Caroline, tell your father what you've been doing today.'

'I've been helping Mummy,' Caroline told him. 'We've been baking things ready for the party tomorrow, cakes and meringues and stuff like that. We've got loads of people coming, at least twenty.'

'Ah, yes . . . the party.' Mr Spruce made a mental note that he must find some excuse to be away from home tomorrow afternoon. Maybe he could fit in a round of golf?

'And Jonathan's been . . .' Mrs Spruce appealed wildly to her son. 'Jonathan, tell your father what you've been doing.'

'Er, nothing much,' said Jonathan. 'I played in the garden for a while by myself.

Oh, and I saw that boy –' He stopped as Caroline kicked him under the table.

'What boy?' asked Mr Spruce.

'Er – a boy from the village.' Jonathan's face turned even pinker. 'You wouldn't know him.'

In panic Mrs Spruce turned to her youngest daughter. 'And you, Charlotte. Tell Daddy what you've been doing.'

'Well . . .' Charley began reluctantly. 'Actually, it's meant to be a secret.'

Jonathan and Caroline smirked at each other.

Charley flushed. 'All right. If you must know, me and – and Someone Else went up to the – to a place I'm not allowed to mention – and – and we found a DUCKODILE!'

Jonathan looked scornful. 'What on earth's a *duckodile?*'

'Well, it's a sort of crocodile . . . but it's got a face like a duck.'

'A sort of crocodile!' Mr Spruce smiled indulgently at his youngest daughter. 'And you weren't afraid?'

She shook her head until the curls bounced. 'It was only a baby one. Please Daddy, could I have a kitten?'

'A kitten?' Mr Spruce was taken aback.

'Now, Charlotte,' intercepted her mother, 'you know very well I won't have animals in the house. Cats are nasty, dirty creatures. They spread all sorts of horrible diseases. Please don't mention the subject again.' She got up from her stool and went to fetch a glass dish full of trifle.

Charley's mouth turned down at the corners. 'But I don't want any old cat. I want a Siamese, like Miss Stokes has got. Its name is So-So and today when I went to her house she let me stroke it.'

At the name of 'Stokes' everyone drew a

sharp breath.

Mr Spruce stared at his daughter. 'Why did you go to Miss Stokes's house?'

'To take his watch back.'

'Whose watch?'

Charley looked suddenly nervous, as if a large pit had opened up in front of her. 'Someone Else's.'

Mrs Spruce raised up the trifle dish she was holding and deliberately dropped it on to the tiled floor. 'Oh, dear,' she said. 'Silly me. Caroline, fetch the squeejy-mop, please. Jonathan, you can bring me a bucket of water — and Charlotte, the dustpan-and-brush. Christopher, I think you'd better leave the room until we've cleared up the mess.' And she pushed her husband out of the door before he had a chance to ask the question clearly hovering on his lips.

Chapter Eight

???????

Sprog sat in the living-room, keeping watch over his sleeping pet.

Suddenly Achilles opened his eyes, blinked twice, and looked about him. The first thing he saw was So-So, crouched on the arm of the chair, her hackles rising and her eyes like blue fire. He tried to move, but his legs were cocooned in blankets. Seized with panic, he thrashed about with his tail, trying to free himself.

Sprog moved swiftly to kneel beside him. 'Don't be scared. So-So's only a cat. She won't harm you.'

Achilles stopped struggling and gazed up at Sprog's face. Had he understood? Sprog tried to pick up his thoughts, but all he could hear was puzzlement, like a long line of question marks. '???????'

'I expect you're wondering where you are,' Sprog said aloud, thinking that even if Achilles didn't understand, the sound of his voice might reassure him. 'Well, you're in Dolphin Cottage, where my Aunt Cis lives. You'll like Aunt Cis. She's gone out to get you some food.'

'???????'

'Baby food, all mashed up like the stuff you'd be eating if you were still in the nest. You've got to have it because you can't chew properly yet, not until your teeth are stronger.'

'???????'

'Teeth.' Sprog opened his mouth and tapped his own. To his delight Achilles drew out one skinny arm from beneath the blanket and tried to copy him. 'You see? They aren't big enough yet. But they will be. When you grow up you'll have dozens and dozens of teeth, just like your mother.'

'???????'

'Your mother.' Sprog conjured up a picture in his mind of Minerva as he had first seen her, coming out of the pool in the cave.

'Mama!' said Achilles.

'That's right! She's very nice. You'd like

her ...' Sprog stopped when he saw two large tears appear in Achilles' eyes; then went on quickly, 'She's not here at the moment, I'm afraid. But don't worry, I'll look after you instead.'

The tears spilled over and ran down Achilles' face to splash on the blanket.

'Oh, please,' said Sprog. 'Don't cry, Achilles.'

'???????'

'Achilles. That's your name.' Glad of the excuse to change the subject, Sprog hurried on, 'Everyone has a name. Mine's Sprog. Well, actually it's Simon Peter Richard Ogden, but everyone calls me Sprog. I'm a human being, you see – and you're a corythosaurus.'

Achilles yawned.

'Yes, I suppose it is rather a long word. Anyway, it doesn't really matter. Do you want to go to sleep again?'

The little dinosaur closed his eyes and snuggled down into the blanket. Sprog sat gazing at him. He couldn't help feeling disappointed that Achilles couldn't talk properly, even in thought language. But then he was only a baby. It was no use expecting him to hold a normal conversation when he'd only just hatched out of the egg.

Soon afterwards Aunt Cis returned. 'Mission accomplished,' she said, setting her bag down on the sofa. 'How's Achilles?'

'Asleep. He woke up for a while and we had a sort of conversation, but then he got rather upset.'

'Why upset?'

'Well ... I mentioned Minerva and it made him cry.' Sprog peered into the bag. 'What did you get?'

'Spinach-and-carrot, cauliflower cheese, vegetable risotto,' she said, reading the labels as she took the jars out of the bag. 'And some delicious prunes-and-custard for afters.'

'Ugh!' said Sprog. 'Sounds disgusting.'

'The choice was somewhat limited. Oh, and I got some rusks for him to chew on. I thought they'd be good for his teeth. Mrs Dobson on the check-out gave me some very funny looks, I can tell you! I didn't have the nerve to ask for nappies as well.'

'Nappies?' He stared at her, aghast. 'You can't put nappies on a dinosaur!'

'Perhaps not,' she agreed, rather reluctantly. 'But it's no use expecting him to be fully house-trained, you know. He's bound to make puddles, like any other baby animal. Go and look if you don't believe me.'

He knelt on the rug and drew the blankets away from the sleeping dinosaur. To his dismay he saw that Aunt Cis was right. Achilles was lying in a pool of dampness – and worse!

'It wouldn't matter if he was still living in the cave,' she went on. 'This is not a natural environment for him.'

'I can soon train him,' Sprog said quickly. 'He's very intelligent.'

'I daresay he is. But it wouldn't be fair to try to make him into a pet.' Before Sprog could argue that this was exactly what he wanted, to keep Achilles as a pet, she continued, 'That's why we need to discuss his future. In the meantime you'd better give him a bath. You can use the kitchen sink.'

'It seems a pity to wake him.'

'He's awake already. Look, he's opened his eyes.'

Disturbed by the sound of voices, Achilles blinked and said, 'Sprog?'

A slow smile spread over Sprog's face. 'He said my name,' he told Aunt Cis, knowing she had been unable to hear it. 'It's his first word. Well, almost his first word.' He was careful not to allow 'Mama' even to enter his head, in case Achilles should get upset again.

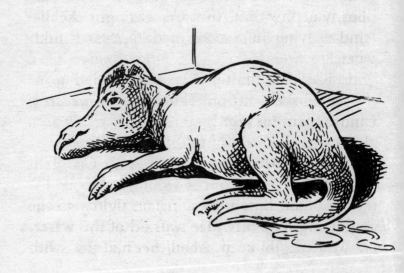

Aunt Cis nodded. 'I expect he'll learn fast, once he starts.'

At the sound of her voice Achilles raised his head and blinked at her. '???????' he enquired.

'That's Aunt Cis,' Sprog said. 'I did tell you about her, do you remember? She went out to buy you some food, but now she's come back and we're going to give you a bath.' He added, before Achilles had time to utter a single question mark, 'That means we're going to put you in some water and wash you all over.'

He picked up the little dinosaur and carried him into the kitchen. Achilles didn't struggle, but looked about him with interest. Aunt Cis put the plug into the sink and ran the hot and cold taps until there was sufficient luke-warm water to cover Achilles' body. Then Sprog began to lower him into it . . .

'Wah-hah!' screamed Achilles in protest – and not in thought language either, but in a loud and clamorous wail. 'Wah-hah!'

'What's the matter?' asked Aunt Cis. 'Is it too hot?'

'No,' said Sprog, hanging on tightly to the wriggling dinosaur. 'He's afraid of the water. It reminds him of when he had to swim through the tunnel to get to the cave and nearly drowned.'

'Oh, dear.' Hastily she rummaged in her bag. 'Here – I bought this. Look, Achilles. It's a little yellow duck. Let's put it in the water and see it float.'

'Wah–' Achilles stopped in mid-yell to stare down at the bobbing plastic duck.

Sprog looked at Aunt Cis and raised his eyebrows.

'I saw it on the shelf,' she explained, rather shamefaced. 'And I thought he might like it to play with. He's only a baby, after all.'

Sprog grinned. 'It looks a bit like him. At least, the face does. Anyway, it seems to be keeping him quiet.'

Fascinated by the little yellow duck, Achilles allowed himself to be lowered into the water and thoroughly washed. He lay there happily, unresisting – until he discovered that if he flicked his tail it made the water splash over the sides of the sink, drenching Sprog and Aunt Cis. A gleam came into his small round eyes. Splash-splash! Splash-splash!

'I'd better take him out,' Sprog said, wiping the water droplets off his face. 'He's nice and clean now, anyway.'

'I'll give you a hand with the drying,' said Aunt Cis.

Between them they managed to lift Achilles onto the kitchen table and rub him down with a towel. By this time he was hungry again so Sprog spooned half a jar of vegetable risotto into his mouth before putting him back on the hearth rug. For a while he lay happily chewing on a rusk; but before long his eyes closed and his mouth dropped open and he began to snore.

Exhausted, Sprog and Aunt Cis sank into armchairs. To Sprog's relief, Aunt Cis said she was too tired to discuss the problem of Achilles' future. 'Tomorrow,' she said. 'We'll talk about it properly tomorrow.'

Chapter Nine

A Full-time Job

Next morning Sprog awoke to find something heavy lying across his legs. 'Get off, So-So,' he muttered. The cat did not move. Sprog reached out a hand to push her away – and instead of fur touched a hard, scaly body.

'Achilles?' He sat up and switched on the lamp. Two small round eyes blinked up at him. 'How did you get here?'

Last night they had left him sleeping in an old dog basket Aunt Cis had found in the barn. They had placed the basket in front of the Aga and closed the kitchen door to make sure he didn't stray. He couldn't possibly have opened the door himself – but So-So could. So-So was a remarkably clever cat who had long ago mastered the art of jumping up to give door handles a nudge.

'So-So must have let you out.' Sprog stroked the little dinosaur's head. 'And you came up the stairs ... and found my room ... and climbed on to my bed.'

'Sprog,' said Achilles.

'You were looking for me!' Sprog felt a warm glow spread through him. Already Achilles knew who he belonged to. He was going to make the perfect pet.

'Food,' said Achilles.

'You're hungry? Okay, I'll get dressed, and then we'll go downstairs.' He picked up his watch, the one Charley Spruce had brought back yesterday. 'It's very early, only five-thirty. Perhaps we should wait a bit.'

'Food, food, food!' Achilles insisted, bouncing up and down on the bed.

'Oh, all right.' Yawning, Sprog climbed out of bed. It was freezing cold and still dark outside. He started to take off his pyjama jacket, but Achilles bounced even harder.

'*Food, food, food!*'

Sprog gave up trying to dress. He shoved his feet into slippers, picked up Achilles and padded downstairs with the dinosaur under his arm. Still half-asleep, he took a jar of prunes-and-custard from the larder and un-screwed the lid.

'FOOD, FOOD, FOOD!' Achilles jumped up and down on the kitchen table, making it shake about on the stone flags. Hurriedly Sprog took a spoon from the drawer and began to shovel prunes-and-custard into Achilles' demanding mouth. Now he knew why his mother used to say that looking after babies was a full-time job. As soon as Achilles had finished eating, Sprog gave him a rusk to keep him quiet.

'Ah, I thought I heard a noise.' Aunt Cis came into the kitchen, her short grey hair still ruffled from sleep. 'Did Achilles get you up early?'

Sprog explained what had happened. 'He's going to take a lot of looking after,' he said, then added quickly, 'But I don't mind. I want to keep him, Aunt Cis. When Mum and Dad come back we're going to live in the country miles from anywhere. Dad says he's had enough of cities. He wants a large garden with plenty of trees to attract the birds . . . and probably a pond as well.' Sprog stroked his pet's scaly back. 'Achilles will love it.'

Aunt Cis looked doubtful. 'Don't you think he might be lonely?'

'Lonely?'

'Remember how you feel when you're away from your family. You can't wait to see them again, can you? You're longing for them to come home.'

'But Achilles doesn't have a family.'

'He has a mother.'

'She's in Loch Ness.' He added, before Aunt Cis could suggest they take Achilles up to Scotland, 'At least that's where we last saw her. But some people think there may be an underwater channel from Loch Ness into the sea which is why they've never been able to find the monster. I read it in a book. That means Minerva could be miles away by now. She could be swimming in the Atlantic Ocean.'

'I doubt it. She's not an aquatic creature. More likely she'll have found a cave to live in.'

Sprog was silent, thinking about Minerva living somewhere in a Scottish cave.

'Mama?' Achilles stopped chewing on the rusk. He raised his head to look inquiringly at Sprog. 'Where's Mama?'

'Miles away,' Sprog repeated, only in thought language. 'Miles and miles.'

Tears sprang into Achilles' eyes. He opened his mouth and wailed, 'Wah-hooo! Wah-hooo!'

'Oh, Lord!' groaned Sprog. 'Quick – where's the plastic duck?'

'Here.' Aunt Cis pushed the duck under Achilles' nose. He stopped wailing at once and took hold of it with his two front claws. 'I think he needs another bath,' she said, wrinkling her nose.

Sprog groaned again, remembering what a messy and exhausting job it had been last night.

'Bath?' Achilles looked up hopefully. 'Water? Splash-splash?'

'He's a quick learner,' Sprog told Aunt Cis. 'He knows quite a lot of words already.'

'Splash-splash!' said Achilles, jumping up and down on the table. 'Splash-splash!'

Much later that morning, when Achilles was bathed and had fallen asleep in his dog basket; and Aunt Cis and Sprog had had time to get dressed and have their own breakfasts; and So-So had been fed; and Sprog had sat down at the table to write the Christmas cards to his family he had felt too tired to write last night, there came a ring at the door bell.

'I'll answer it,' said Aunt Cis. 'You stay here and keep an eye on Achilles.'

Sprog went to listen at the kitchen door. He recognized Mrs Spruce's voice at once. She sounded hesitant and anxious.

'. . . a very great favour,' she was saying to Aunt Cis. 'Oh, dear, I don't quite know how to put this, but – well, I'd be so grateful if you didn't tell my husband that your great-nephew's staying with you over Christmas. It's just that I – er, we – er –'

'You don't have to explain,' said Aunt Cis. 'I understand perfectly.'

Sprog opened the door a crack. Looking down the hall he could see not only Mrs Spruce but also Jonathan and Caroline, hovering close behind her. There was no sign of Charley.

'Of course,' Mrs Spruce went on, 'it might be awkward if they met in the village . . .'

'You needn't worry,' said Aunt Cis. 'Sprog's having to stay indoors at the moment. He's – er, caught something.'

'Caught something? You mean a virus?' Mrs Spruce shrank back. She spread out her arms like a barrier, as if to protect Jonathan and Caroline from any germs that might be waiting to pounce. 'Oh dear, I hope it's nothing serious?'

'No, but you can rest assured your husband is unlikely to bump into him over the holiday. Goodbye, Mrs Spruce.'

Aunt Cis closed the front door firmly and returned to the kitchen.

'Did you hear?' she asked Sprog.

He nodded. 'You were brilliant. I especially liked it when you said I'd caught something. Meaning Achilles, I suppose?'

'I always try not to lie if I can possibly help it.' Aunt Cis looked apologetic. 'But I'm afraid this means you won't be able to go out much.'

'I don't mind that. I'd rather stay here and look after Achilles anyway.' He grinned. 'I've got a feeling that dinosaur-sitting is going to be a full-time job.'

Achilles opened his eyes and blinked. He sat up in the basket and said, 'Splash-splash.'

'He's changed his mind about water,' Sprog said. 'He likes it now.'

'There's an old tin bath out in the barn,' said Aunt Cis. 'Why don't you fill it up and let him play out there? If I keep the car in the drive for the time being you can make the barn into a dinosaur-nursery. Then he can splash around as much as he likes.'

'Sounds great.' Sprog directed his thoughts to Achilles, conjuring up a picture in his mind of a tin bath filled with water. 'Would you like that, Achilles?'

'Splash-splash!' Achilles jumped eagerly out of the basket.

Chapter Ten

A Little Gentle Bribery

While his wife and two older children were out of the house Mr Spruce sat in his study, trying to read the newspaper. But he found it hard to concentrate. His mind kept straying to other things. In the end he gave up and went in search of his youngest daughter.

He found her kneeling up at the kitchen table, drawing on a large sheet of paper. 'Charlotte,' he began, 'when you said yesterday that you'd called at Dolphin Cottage to "take back his watch," whose watch were you talking about?'

'I told you,' said Charley. 'It was Someone Else's.'

'Yes, but who *is* this Someone Else?'

'I can't say.' She bent over the paper, sticking her tongue out with the effort of concentration. She was good at drawing: even her teacher said so.

Mr Spruce decided to try a little gentle bribery. 'Charlotte dear, how would you like something special for Christmas? An extra present, just for you alone?'

She looked up at him in astonishment. 'Me alone? Not Jonathan or Caroline?'

'That's right. Anything you like. A new doll, perhaps? Or a –' He broke off, staring down at her drawing. 'What on earth's that supposed to be?'

'It's a duckodile.' She gave her father a long, considering look. 'You know what I want. I want a kitten.'

'Now you heard what your mother said yesterday. She won't have animals in the house because they're dirty. What's a duckodile?'

'I told you, it's a baby crocodile with a face like a duck. Cats aren't dirty and they keep the mice away. Mummy *hates* mice.'

'We don't have any mice.' Mr Spruce bent closer to inspect the drawing. 'You know, it looks remarkably like a – Well, never mind what it looks like. Where exactly did you see this – er, duckodile?'

'In a cave.

'Which cave?'

'Dragon's Tooth.' She added quickly, 'But it doesn't live there any more. Someone took it . . . somewhere else.'

'Where?'

'I don't know. You'll have to be quick if you want to buy me a kitten. It must be a Siamese kitten like So-So, and it's already Christmas Eve.'

'Just tell me where and I'll buy you a kitten this afternoon.' Mr Spruce fixed his daughter with a challenging look.

'It's our party this afternoon.'

'I don't mind missing it.' He'd be glad of the excuse to go out. Anything rather than stay in a house full of other people's children playing noisy games and stuffing themselves with sausage rolls. 'So where's this ... this duckodile now?'

For a long moment Charley hesitated. Then she said, 'At Miss Stokes's.'

'Ah!' A look of extreme satisfaction crossed Mr Spruce's face.

The barn made an ideal dinosaur-nursery. There was plenty of room once the Morris had been driven out; and all the tools for the garden or the car were hung on hooks or stored on shelves, well out of Achilles' reach. Aunt Cis had even removed the lawnmower, which meant there was nothing valuable he could damage. He could move about as freely as if he were in the cave, jumping in and out of the tin bath whenever he wanted.

After lunch – a picnic in the barn – Sprog carried Achilles up the rickety steps leading to the hayloft. 'This is where Talker lives,' he said.

'Talker?' queried Achilles.

'Talker Harris. He's away at the moment, but when he's at home he sleeps up here. That's his bed, and these are the tea-chests where he keeps all his possessions. Mind you,

87

it doesn't usually look as tidy as this,' he added, noticing the neatly-folded blankets on the low camp bed where Talker slept. Usually they were all in a heap and Talker buried somewhere underneath. He wished the old man were here now – and yet perhaps it was a good thing he wasn't. When they had brought Minerva down from the cave to hide in the barn poor old Talker had been so scared he had insisted on sleeping on the back seat of the car. Sprog grinned to himself.

'Mama?' Achilles twisted his head round to stare into Sprog's face. 'Where's Mama?'

Oh, no! He'd been careless again, letting his thoughts drift to the subject he must at all costs avoid. 'Look, Achilles,' he said, carrying him over to the window. 'You can see for miles from here, right over the village. See that big, square house with the new-looking roof? That's where the Spruces live.'

'Mama lives there?'

'No, I just told you, it's the Spruces' house.' He noticed there were a lot of cars in the drive and people getting out of them, mostly children. 'Oh, I'd forgotten. They're having a party.'

'Party?'

'Lots of things to eat and drink. I wasn't invited, thank goodness. I don't expect it'll be much fun.' He spotted a large, burly figure hurrying away from the house. 'Hello, there's Mr Spruce. I wonder where he's going?'

'Grrrr!' said Achilles, curling back his top lip.

Sprog looked at him, surprised. 'You don't like him? Oh, I suppose you picked up my thoughts again. But you're right, he's our enemy. You must never let him see you, Achilles, because he could be dangerous. Do you understand?'

'Enemy!' muttered Achilles, glaring out of the window.

'That's funny. He's walking down the road. Usually he goes *everywhere* by car.' Sprog pressed his nose against the glass, trying to follow Mr Spruce's progress. 'Perhaps he's going to the shops. No, he's walked past the shops. He's coming in this direction. Oh Lord, he's stopped outside our gate!'

He dodged back quickly in case Mr Spruce should look up at the barn window. Why had he come to Dolphin Cottage? Could Charley have said something to make him suspicious? There must be a reason . . .

He carried Achilles down the steps and set

him on the ground. 'I'm going to find out what's happening. You stay here, there's a good boy.'

'Good boy come too?' said Achilles anxiously, watching him open the side door of the barn.

'I shan't be long, I promise.' Sprog closed the door firmly behind him and dropped the latch. 'Don't you dare let him out,' he told So-So, who was crouching on the garden path. She assured him she had no intention of letting the creature out: last night she had only opened the kitchen door because she wanted a little peace and quiet.

He crept along the side of the house, bending low so that he could not be seen from the road. Taking cover behind a lavender bush he peered round at the front path, then drew back hastily as he heard Mr Spruce's loud voice booming on the doorstep.

'Ah, Miss Stokes. Sorry to bother you, but my daughter has asked me for a kitten for Christmas and it seems she's set her heart on having one like yours. A Siamese, isn't it? I'd be glad if you could tell me where you got it.'

'I can certainly tell you, though it may not be of much help.' Aunt Cis sounded decidedly frosty. 'So-So had been neglected by her previous owners and was taken by a neighbour to Mr Hogben, the vet. He treated her until she was well again and then offered her to me, knowing I would give her a good home.'

'Ah, the vet! I'll call and ask him straight away.'

'But I warn you, even if he does know of a Siamese kitten, he won't approve of you giving one as a present. Cats, like dogs, aren't just for Christmas.'

'Of course not. I realize that.' Mr Spruce suddenly put on a concerned voice. 'How are you, Miss Stokes? Not too lonely, I hope.'

'I'm never lonely, thank you, Mr Spruce.'

'I see you've left your car in the drive. Not wise, you know, this weather. Better to keep it in the barn.'

Sprog drew in his breath. Surely Mr Spruce couldn't have guessed the real reason for the car being in the drive?

'I intend to use it later,' said Aunt Cis. 'Goodbye, Mr Spruce.'

The door slammed shut. Footsteps sounded down the path. The gate squeaked.

Cautiously Sprog raised his head to look over the lavender bush. He saw Mr Spruce stop at the end of the drive and stare back at Dolphin Cottage with a frown of deep suspicion on his large red face; then start walking slowly and thoughtfully back up the road towards his house.

Chapter Eleven

Intruder!

'A Siamese kitten!' Sprog said with disgust. 'Of all the feeble excuses! I reckon he came to spy on us.' He stroked the head of Achilles, who lay in his basket on the kitchen floor, chewing on a rusk.

'We'll have to be careful from now on,' said Aunt Cis. 'I'm afraid that all the time Achilles stays here he may be in danger.'

'As soon as Mum and Dad come home it'll be okay,' Sprog said confidently. 'Then we can take him with us to our new house.'

Aunt Cis said nothing; but her face said clearly she doubted it would be as simple as that.

So-So, who had been washing herself on the window-sill, took a flying leap on to the table and pushed urgently against Aunt Cis's hand. Sprog looked up and said, 'I think there's somebody outside.'

He covered Achilles with the blanket and went to open the back door. A guilty-looking Charlotte Spruce stood on the step, her face flushed and tear-stained. Beneath her outdoor coat, hastily dragged on and buttoned unevenly, showed the skirt of a pale blue party dress.

Sprog glowered at her. 'What do you want?' he demanded.

'I came to tell you—' she began; then stopped. Her lip quivered and her nose turned pink. 'I didn't say anything, honestly I didn't.

But I did a drawing . . . of the – of the –' She tried to see past him to Achilles' basket.

'Of the duckodile,' Sprog said helpfully.

'Yes. And Daddy was ever so interested. He asked where I'd seen it and I told him Dragon's Tooth Cave. And then he asked where it was now and I – I –' She flushed even pinker. 'Well, he promised to buy me a kitten.'

'A Siamese kitten?' enquired Aunt Cis.

'Yes.' She bent to stroke So-So, who had come to rub against her legs. 'Mummy won't let us have any pets, you see. But if Daddy buys me a kitten she'll have to let me keep it, won't she?'

Sprog's anger began to fade. She wasn't such a bad kid, really: by far the best of her family. 'It's okay,' he said gruffly.

'You're not cross with me?'

'Only a bit.' Well, he had to be truthful.

A beaming smile spread over her face. 'Can I stay here and play with So-So?'

'Aren't you supposed to be at the party?'

'Yes, but it isn't any fun. They're mostly Jonathan and Caroline's friends from school and they keep bossing me around. I'd much rather stay here.'

'Better not,' said Aunt Cis. 'Your mother

95

may miss you and send some people out to search for you. We don't want to risk that,' she added, with a meaning look at Sprog.

'No, we don't,' he agreed. 'Sorry, Charley. You'll have to go.'

Her face fell. 'Oh, all right.' Reluctantly she turned away. 'Promise you're not cross with me, Sprog?'

'I promise,' he said, and firmly closed the door. He turned to Aunt Cis. 'Sounds like old Spruce is getting suspicious. It might be safer if Achilles stays in the barn tonight. I'll sleep upstairs in the loft, on Talker's bed.'

And Aunt Cis, being Aunt Cis and not like other people's aunts, merely said, 'Better take your quilt and two hot-water bottles, otherwise you'll freeze to death.' She added, 'I take it you won't be coming with me to the midnight service?'

He shook his head. 'I daren't leave Achilles. Besides, I might bump into Mr Spruce.'

'Very likely. I must go, of course, because I'm playing the organ. Sure you won't mind being here alone?'

'Not a bit,' he assured her.

'Good night, Achilles.' Sprog tucked in the blanket round the sides of the basket and patted the little dinosaur on the head. 'Don't worry, I shan't be far away, just at the top of those steps.'

'Me too?' asked Achilles hopefully.

Sprog hesitated. He was tempted to take the basket up to the hayloft and put it beside him on the floor; but he guessed that if he did that Achilles would only try to join him on the bed, which was far too narrow for two. He said firmly, 'No, you stay here. Go to sleep, there's a good boy.'

'Good boy,' Achilles repeated happily. He yawned and wriggled down beneath his blanket.

Sprog climbed into the loft. Brrr! It was even colder up here than down in the barn. He was glad he was already wearing his pyjamas and dressing-gown: getting un-dressed would have been a chilly business.

At the top of the steps he found the switch and turned off the single electric light bulb suspended from the rafters. Now he was in the dark – and oh, drat! he had forgotten to bring the torch with him. Well, he couldn't be bothered to go and fetch it. Cautiously he groped his way across the uneven floor. He stubbed his toe on a packing-case and fell on to the bed, stifling his groans. It was far too cold to take off his dressing-gown: better keep it on all night. And his slippers.

Beneath the quilt, however, he discovered a glorious little nest of warmth, thanks to Aunt Cis who had put the two hot-water bottles into the bed half-an-hour ago. He burrowed into it and determinedly closed his eyes.

At first it seemed very quiet – and to be honest, rather spooky. Although it was still quite early in the evening, about nine-thirty, he found it hard to relax, and nearly jumped out of his skin when he heard an extraordinary noise, halfway between an express train and a dying pig – until he realized that it was Achilles snoring! Now he knew why poor So-so had let him out of the kitchen last night to give herself some peace and quiet. He pulled the quilt over his ears to shut it out and soon afterwards fell asleep.

Suddenly he awoke with a start. Was that a noise he'd heard? He sat up in bed, listening hard. Yes, there it was again! A stealthy footstep on the gravel drive.

Someone was prowling around the barn.

He swung his legs off the bed and stood up, his heart thumping. If only he had remembered the torch! He would have to find the light switch. Cautiously he groped his way across the loft towards the steps.

Just as he reached the top he heard another noise. Someone had lifted the catch on the side door. It creaked as it swung open, letting in a blast of cold night air. Sprog froze, his hand on the light switch, as he watched a torch-beam travel across the floor, moving so swiftly over Achilles' basket that for a moment it seemed to have missed it. But then the beam returned, as if for a second look, and this time it woke Achilles. Startled, he raised his head.

The intruder uttered a sharp exclamation.

Mr Spruce? But it hadn't sounded like his voice. Although there was something strangely familiar . . .

'Stone me!' said the intruder. 'Reckon I must have had a drop too many.'

'Talker?' Sprog switched on the light.

The barn was instantly illuminated. Sure enough, there stood Talker Harris, in his old patched jacket with the lampshade fringe around the bottom, staring at Achilles with a look of stunned bewilderment on his face. Achilles, equally alarmed at the sight of the gaunt old man with straggly grey hair and drooping moustache, began to struggle out of his basket.

'A dragon!' Talker said incredulously. He took a step backwards, raising his hands as if to protect himself. 'It's another flaming dragon!'

'Talker, don't be scared.' Sprog nearly fell down the steps in his haste. 'His name's Achilles and he's Minerva's son.'

But Talker was in no mood to listen to explanations. He waved his arms wildly at Achilles, who was crawling across the floor towards him. 'Get away from me, you beast! Get away!' And when Achilles, not understanding, continued to advance, Talker fled through the open doorway and down the drive, yelling at the top of his voice, 'A dragon! *Another* flaming dragon!'

'Talker, come back!' Sprog pulled the door shut and set off in pursuit, desperate to catch him before he could tell the entire village what he had just seen. 'Talker, wait!'

Neither of them noticed the large, burly figure of a man lurking behind the lavender bush. As soon as they had run into the road he detached himself from the shadows and crept stealthily towards the barn.

Chapter Twelve

Kidnapped

At this hour on any other winter's night the streets of Silverton would have been deserted, the villagers fast asleep in their beds. But it was Christmas Eve and most of them had been to the midnight service. As they came streaming out of the church and down the path, who should they see but Talker Harris, with his long grey hair and fringed jacket, racing down the road towards them. 'A dragon! Another flaming dragon!' they heard him shout and everyone burst out laughing.

'Good old Talker, up to his tricks again.'

'Nice to have him back. Life's been dull without him.'

'Seeing dragons, indeed! Reckon he's been celebrating his return at the George.' They cheered as he sprinted past them.

'Happy Christmas, Talker!'

Sprog, following close behind, suddenly realized that if he went any further he would be clearly visible in the light coming from the open church door – and he was only wearing his dressing-gown and slippers. He slithered to a halt and took cover behind a pillar box. The organ was still playing, which meant that Aunt Cis was still inside. If he told her what had happened, with luck she might be able to stop Talker telling the entire village what he had seen.

He climbed over the wall and ran across the churchyard, picking his way between the gravestones. The big oak door stood open but the flood of people coming out had slowed to a trickle. The church must be nearly empty now. Keeping as far as possible in the shadows he slipped into the porch – and walked straight into the Spruce family.

'Hello, Sprog!' said Charley, looking surprised and pleased.

'Oh, my heavens!' exclaimed Mrs Spruce. 'What are you doing out of bed, you silly boy? Jonathan, run straight back inside and tell Miss Stokes that her nephew is delirious. He's walking in his sleep.'

Jonathan disappeared at once. Caroline

remarked, 'It's a good thing Daddy isn't with us.'

'It is indeed!' Mrs Spruce agreed fervently.

Sprog was equally relieved. The last person he wanted to meet at this particular moment was Mr Spruce.

'Daddy's got a headache,' Charley informed him. She leaned forward to add confidentially, 'Least, that's what he said. *I* think he stayed at home to look after my kitten.'

'Charlotte, keep back!' her mother commanded. 'I don't want you catching any nasty germs.'

Inside the church the organ stopped abruptly, right in the middle of a chord, and

ten seconds later Aunt Cis appeared in the doorway, followed by Jonathan. 'What's happened?' she asked Sprog.

'Talker's home,' he told her. 'He came into the barn and – er, had a bit of a shock. Now he's gone down the road yelling his head off.' He shivered, for the first time aware that his dressing-gown was too thin to keep out the cold night air.

'That child should be in bed,' Mrs Spruce told Aunt Cis sternly. 'He's clearly running a temperature.'

'Yes, indeed,' Aunt Cis agreed. 'Sprog, go home.'

'What about Talker?'

'I'll take care of Talker, don't worry.'

As he started down the path he heard Aunt Cis thanking Mrs Spruce for her concern. Charley's voice called after him, 'Happy Christmas, Sprog,' and he managed a rather half-hearted 'Happy Christmas,' in reply. In truth he felt anything but happy. He had wanted Talker to come home, yet now the old man was here it seemed he had brought nothing but trouble.

And there was worse to come. Far, far worse. When he reached Dolphin Cottage he found the barn still lit but empty and the side door open. 'Achilles?' he called. 'Achilles, where are you?'

There was no reply. Not even a snore. Only silence.

'I expect he came looking for me,' Sprog said miserably to Aunt Cis when at last she returned with Talker. 'And somehow he must have got lost.'

'He can't have gone far,' she said. 'I expect he's somewhere in the garden.'

Sprog shook his head. 'I've searched it over and over. There's no sign of him.'

'It'll be easier when it's daylight. We'll soon find him then.' She glanced at Talker, who had slumped into the high-back chair beside the Aga. 'I think what we all need now is a mug of hot tea.'

'Huh!' Talker muttered resentfully. 'A person comes home from his wanderings, expecting some sort of a welcome – and what does he find? An outbreak of dragons!'

'If you'd given us some warning you were coming,' Aunt Cis said tartly, 'we'd have hung out the flags.'

'It's Christmas, ain't it? You know I always come home for Christmas.'

'Well, you did leave it a little late this year.

Indeed, you couldn't have left it much later.' Her expression softened as she put some chocolate digestive biscuits – Talker's favourite – on a plate. 'Still, we're glad to see you now that you're here. Aren't we, Sprog?'

'Mmmm, yes.' But it was hard to sound enthusiastic when his heart was heavy as lead. How could he have been so careless as to leave that side door open? The strange thing was that he could have sworn he closed it behind him when he ran after Talker. Perhaps the catch had not dropped properly . . .

He swung round to look at So-So, who was curled up on the rug at Talker's feet. 'Was it you?' he asked her in thought language. 'Did you help him escape?'

She opened one eye and told him that she had never left the kitchen all night. She had heard everything, though, the whole commotion. Talker shouting, and Sprog chasing after him, and then the stranger.

'Stranger? What stranger?' asked Sprog.

What she told him next made his blood run cold. He turned to Aunt Cis, who was handing a mug of tea to Talker. 'So-so says that after I'd left she heard someone's footsteps on the drive . . . and the barn door creak open.'

Aunt Cis sat down facing him. 'Are you thinking what I'm thinking?' she asked.

He took the mug in his hands, not because he wanted to drink – he didn't even like tea – but for its comforting warmth. 'Mr Spruce wasn't in church tonight.'

'I noticed that. I can see a lot from the organ loft.'

'Charley said he stayed at home because he had a headache.'

'That's possible, I suppose. But in the circumstances I can't help finding it rather suspicious.' Aunt Cis looked grave. 'What if he's decided to get his own back? After all, you once kidnapped him to take him to Minerva's cave . . .'

'And now he's kidnapped Achilles in return.' Sprog groaned. 'I should never have left the barn.'

'Well, it's no use reproaching yourself,' Aunt Cis said in a bracing tone. 'What's done is done. Tomorrow morning, when our brains are fresher, we'll work out a plan of action.' She drained her mug and stood up. 'Talker, you can have your old bed in the hayloft. Sprog may as well sleep in his own room tonight.'

Sprog got up reluctantly. 'Don't you think

I should stay in the barn? Supposing Achilles wasn't kidnapped? Supposing he comes back?'

'Talker will let us know soon enough. Try to get a good night's sleep – or rather, what's left of it.'

But Sprog found it impossible to sleep. He kept thinking of poor Achilles and how scared the little dinosaur must be. If he concentrated hard perhaps he could pick up his thoughts. He tried, but could hear nothing, only a great empty silence. There must be too much distance between them. Perhaps tomorrow, if he could get nearer to where Achilles was being held, he might do better.

Tomorrow . . .

Chapter Thirteen

Radar

Charlotte Spruce awakened early next morning and lay in bed shivering, not with cold but with excitement. Christmas morning – and somewhere in the house was hidden her extra-special present! The present her father had promised to buy for her alone. A Siamese kitten.

She was longing to see it. She tried to picture that moment after breakfast when they all sat round the Christmas tree and unwrapped their parcels. Not that the kitten would come in a parcel, of course. It would most likely be in a basket with a bright red ribbon tied around its neck. Oh, she could hardly wait . . .

She *couldn't* wait! She flung back the quilt, jumped out of bed and pulled on her dressing-gown. It was still dark outside and the house was silent: everyone else must be fast asleep. She opened the door, taking care not to make a sound. The landing light was left on all night – Jonathan was afraid of the dark – so it was easy to find her way down the stairs. Where would the kitten be hidden? Somewhere safe. Somewhere nobody was likely to look. Somewhere it couldn't be heard if it mewed . . .

Her father's study! Nobody was allowed in there in case they disturbed his notes for the book he was writing about dental hygiene. What better place to hide something he didn't want anyone to find?

She crept along to the door at the farthest end of the hall and tried the handle. It was locked. That was strange: even though the room was out of bounds it wasn't usually kept locked. A muffled sound caught her attention: she put her ear to the door, listening hard. Yes, there was definitely something inside! Something alive. She could hear it making a funny little noise. Not mewing. It sounded more like snoring.

She tried the handle again. Oh, fiddle! Well, at least she knew where it was. She knew that her father hadn't forgotten. Only

another hour or so and she would be holding it in her arms, her own sweet little furry kitten.

Reluctantly she climbed the stairs and returned to her room to wait.

'Happy Christmas,' Aunt Cis said sadly when Sprog came downstairs for breakfast.

'Happy Christmas,' he replied in an equally gloomy tone. This must surely be the worst Christmas of his life. No family, no presents . . . and now no Achilles.

'Hungry?'

He shook his head.

'At least have something to drink.' She poured orange juice from a carton into a glass and handed it to him. 'Did you manage to sleep?'

'Not much.' He bent to pat So-So's head, then sank on to a chair. 'I was too worried about Achilles. What do you think Mr Spruce will do with him?'

'That's been puzzling me too.' Aunt Cis stirred her tea. 'I've tried to put myself in his place. Think the way he would think. Although I must confess it isn't easy.'

'How do you think he would think?' Sprog asked.

'Well, I imagine he wants to prove to everyone, not only his family, that he isn't mad. That he was telling the truth when he said he'd seen a dinosaur. Which means that now he's got Achilles he will want to show him off to as many people as possible.'

Sprog groaned. 'You think he might go on television again, like he did when he took Minerva's tooth out?'

'Perhaps. But not until he's made quite certain that Achilles is really a corythosaurus. He won't want to risk looking foolish a second time. No, I suspect he'll try to get a second opinion.'

'Who from?'

'A dinosaur expert, I suppose, if there is such a thing.'

Sprog began to feel more hopeful. He reached for a slice of toast. 'That means he won't start showing Achilles off straight away. We may still have time to rescue him.'

'The question is, how?'

He said slowly, 'Last night I kept thinking – if I could get close enough to Achilles I might be able to pick up his thoughts.'

'Like radar, you mean?'

'Yes, like radar. Then I'd know exactly where Mr Spruce is keeping him prisoner.' He buttered the toast and spread it with honey.

'Good idea. Meantime . . .' Aunt Cis sat up straight and braced her shoulders . . . 'I suggest we try to behave as if this were a normal Christmas Day. I've already stuffed the turkey and put it in the oven.'

Sprog sniffed. 'I thought I could smell something good.'

'And soon I shall put the pudding on to steam.' She turned round in her chair to take an envelope off the dresser. 'You had your present yesterday, I'm afraid, but here's a card.'

'I've got something for you as well.' He fished in his dressing-gown pocket and brought out the pencil-and-pen set he had bought her. 'Sorry, I didn't have time to wrap it up.'

'It doesn't matter.' She looked pleased. 'I've been wanting a decent pen for ages.'

He opened the envelope and took out a card with a robin on it and a group of choir-boys singing 'We wish you a merry Christmas'. 'Thanks,' he said; although he knew Christmas couldn't possibly be merry until Achilles was safe home again. He swallowed the remains of the toast and got to his feet. 'Before I go out I'd better look inside the barn, just in case. Shall I take Talker a cup of tea?'

'If I were you I'd let him sleep,' said Aunt Cis. 'Talker unconscious is a lot safer than Talker babbling on about dragons.'

He found the barn still empty. Only the dog basket and the tin bath remained to show that it had ever been home to a baby dinosaur. Sprog climbed the steps and peered into the hayloft. All he could see of Talker was a mound of blankets, gently rising and falling. He left the barn as quietly as he had come, closing the side door behind him.

Right, then. He took a deep breath. There was nothing for it but to go to the Spruces' house and try to find Achilles by 'radar'.

He took the short cut across Samson's field, stopping on the way to ask the old horse if he had seen anything suspicious last night. Yes, Samson told him – a man carrying a small bundle. But it had been dark and his eyes weren't what they used to be. Only his sense of smell had told him that the bundle had been some kind of living creature. Sprog thanked him for his help and walked on.

He came to the fence at the end of the Spruces' garden and looked over. Nobody was about. Most likely they were still unwrapping their presents. Cautiously he went through the gate and took cover behind a holly bush. Now, where was the most likely place?

Once before, on a previous visit, he had found Charley imprisoned inside a garden shed. She had shut herself in by accident and he had rescued her. Supposing Mr Spruce had decided the shed would make a good hiding-place for a dinosaur? Stealthily Sprog made his way across the garden to the side of the house. Yes, there was the shed. He peered through the dusty window, but could see nothing except gardening tools, a mower and a roller. Certainly nothing that moved.

Time to use the radar. He stood still and tried to concentrate. It wasn't easy. His mind kept filling up with stupid, unimportant little thoughts, such as wishing he'd catcn more breakfast because he was now feeling hungry. And wishing he'd done Aunt Cis's present up properly because he'd had plenty of wrapping paper. Masses and masses of it. Paper everywhere, in little bits and pieces . . .

Hang on! Perhaps these weren't his own thoughts? Perhaps he was picking up what Achilles was thinking? Hungry. Yes, he would be hungry by now. He hadn't had his early-morning feed. But paper . . . where did paper come into it?

Sprog moved closer to the side of the house. There was only one window on the ground floor. Not a large window. It looked as if it belonged to a small room, like a store-room or an office. Bending low, he crept along the wall until he was directly beneath it, then cautiously raised his head to look over the sill . . .

Chapter Fourteen

A Raging Monster

Charley couldn't understand it. They had eaten their breakfast and unwrapped their presents and now her father was sitting in his armchair, looking extraordinarily pleased with himself. But he hadn't said a word about the kitten. She was trying hard to be patient. After all, this was an extra present for her alone, so perhaps he didn't want to make too much fuss about it in front of Jonathan and Caroline. But surely she had waited long enough?

She went over to him and said in a low voice, 'You can give it to me now.'

He smiled at her and said, 'Give you what, my precious?' He was certainly in a good mood: he hardly ever called her 'his precious'.

'You know. My special present.' And when he still looked blank she leaned closer to whisper in his ear, 'My kitten.'

'Oh, that. Sorry, Charlotte, but – um, I'm afraid it hasn't been possible. I did ask the vet if he knew where I could get hold of one, but he said there were none available. In any case I'm not sure it was such a good idea. You know how your mother feels about cats.'

She stared at him in shocked disbelief. He was teasing her. He *must* be! 'But you've already got it,' she said. 'I know you have. It's in your study. I came down early this morning and heard it through the door.'

His good mood disappeared in an instant, his kindly Christmas-morning face replaced by a thunderous frown. 'You've been listening at my study door?'

'Yes – and I heard it snoring. And just before breakfast I listened again and I heard it jumping around and knocking things over. So I know it's in there!'

Her father looked alarmed. 'Did you say knocking things over?'

'Yes, it was making a terrible racket.'

He sprang to his feet and rushed out of the room. The rest of his family took no notice: his wife was busy clearing up the discarded wrapping paper while Jonathan played with his new computer game and Caroline with her Walkman.

Charley ran after him. She caught him up as he was unlocking the study door. 'Stay there,' he commanded. 'You can't come in.'

'Oh, but –'

'Do as I say and don't argue!'

He disappeared into his den. Next moment she heard him say something extremely rude . . . and then there was the most awful commotion, as if he was chasing something round and round the room, bumping into furniture and knocking things over. Charley could bear the suspense no longer. She pushed open the door and looked inside.

'Oh!' she exclaimed.

The room was in a state of chaos. Chairs upturned, lamps knocked over – and her father's notes for his book on dental hygiene had been shredded into tiny pieces and tossed all over the place. In the midst of this chaos Mr Spruce lay spreadeagled on the floor, clasping to his chest a small, lively and strangely familiar-looking creature.

'Oh, it's a duckodile,' Charley said, her voice flat with disappointment. 'You got me a duckodile instead of a kitten.'

'Confounded thing!' gasped Mr Spruce, red in the face from the struggle. 'It was so quiet last night . . . half asleep . . . now it's turned into a – a raging monster!'

Certainly at this moment the duckodile appeared far more like a monster than a pet, its little round eyes screwed up with fury and its tail lashing wildly in the air.

'Oh, well,' said Charley, trying to make the best of it, 'I'd have liked a kitten, but of course if you couldn't get me one . . .'

'The vet!' gasped Mr Spruce. 'Fetch the vet!'

'You mean Mr Hogben?'

'Of course I mean Mr Hogben! Tell him I need his help.' Mr Spruce fought to get a better arm-hold. 'Ask him to bring a hypodermic syringe . . . or one of those guns they use to fire darts into rhinos . . . anything to knock this creature unconscious.' He glared up at her. 'Hurry, Charlotte! I can't hold on much longer.'

Reluctantly she turned away.

'And when you've closed the door, put up the "DO NOT DISTURB" sign.'

A bit late for that, Charlotte thought as she obeyed him. The study had been disturbed enough already. What a mess! No doubt her father had thought he was being kind, but she would much rather have had a kitten. A duckodile might be more unusual but it wasn't exactly cuddly.

And heaven knows what her mother was going to say!

She sighed deeply as she walked along the hall and let herself out of the front door.

Sprog, who had been crouched beneath the study window, saw her going down the path and chased after her. 'What's happening?' he demanded.

'Daddy couldn't get me a kitten for Christmas,' Charley said crossly, 'so he's bought me a duckodile instead. You know, one of those things that you've got.'

'It's the same one,' Sprog said with some bitterness.

Her eyes opened wide with surprise. 'Did you sell it to him?'

'No, I didn't! He stole it from me.'

'Don't be silly.' She unlatched the front gate. 'My daddy doesn't steal things.'

'Well, he's stolen Achilles. Last night he came and took him from our barn.'

She shook her head obstinately. 'This is a different duckodile. It's not as nice as yours. This one's really wild.'

'I expect he's hungry.' He followed her through the gate. 'Charley, where are you going?'

'To fetch the vet.'

'The vet?' He was filled with alarm. 'Why – is Achilles ill? I mean the duckodile.'

'No, I don't think he's ill, but he's made an awful mess of Daddy's study. There's paper everywhere.'

'Yes, I know. I saw it through the window. But why does your father want the vet?'

'He needs his help.' She started down the

road. 'I've got to hurry.'

His help? The reason came to Sprog in a flash. Mr Spruce must be seeking a second opinion, just as Aunt Cis had said. The vet might not be a dinosaur expert, but he should be able to recognize a prehistoric animal when he saw one. And if he were to back up Mr Spruce's story . . .

'Charley, wait!' Sprog ran to catch her up. 'I'll fetch the vet. You go home.'

She hesitated. 'If I go home too soon Daddy might be cross.'

'Then don't let him see you for a while. Keep out of his way.' He added persuasively, 'You can play with your presents instead. I expect you had a lot of presents?'

'Yes, I did. Lots and lots.' She was clearly tempted to accept his offer. 'And it's cold out here.'

'Freezing. Much nicer to play in the warm.' As she turned away he warned, 'Better not say you've seen me or your mother will be cross. She doesn't want your father to know I'm here.'

She nodded and ran back into the house.

Now what? Sprog had only the vaguest plan in his head as he raced down the road to Dolphin Cottage. One thing was certain, though: he had no intention of fetching the vet. At least, not the real vet. What he needed was a substitute. After all, this was Christmas Day: it shouldn't be too difficult to persuade Mr Spruce that Mr Hogben was off-duty and had sent someone else in his place.

But who?

He couldn't do it himself, that was obvious. He was far too young and even if he wore a disguise Mr Spruce might recognize him. He'd be sure to recognize Aunt Cis too.

No, there was only one possible person . . .

Chapter Fifteen

The Substitute

'Sit still, Talker, for goodness' sake!' said Aunt Cis, brandishing a large pair of dressmaking scissors. 'I'm not going to hurt you.'

But Talker, seated on a wooden chair in the middle of the kitchen, regarded her with deep mistrust. 'It's taken months to grow me hair this long,' he grumbled. 'And now you're wanting to cut it all off. A right fool I shall look and no mistake.'

'No, you won't,' Sprog assured him. 'You'll look like a vet.'

'In my opinion it'll be an improvement.' Aunt Cis snipped away ruthlessly at Talker's untidy grey locks. 'In fact I've wanted to do this for years.'

Mournfully he watched wisps of his hair floating down to the floor. 'I wouldn't mind so much if I knew what was going on,' he muttered. 'Why do I have to look like a vet?'

'Because when you get to the Spruces' house,' Sprog explained for at least the third time, 'you're going to tell Mr Spruce that you're Mr Hogben's substitute. And when you get into his study you're going to pick up Achilles and pass him through the window to me. I shall be waiting outside. It's dead simple really.'

'I'm not picking up no dragons,' Talker growled. 'I draw the line at picking up dragons.'

'All right, just open the window and I'll climb in and get him. That'll be even simpler.'

Talker said rebelliously, 'You made me wear a disguise one time before, when we did that kidnapping job. Old man Spruce saw through it then and I wouldn't mind betting he'll see through it this time. He'll know soon enough I ain't no vet.'

'Ah, but this time we're not making you wear a disguise,' said Aunt Cis. 'All we're doing is smartening you up. You might even say that we're revealing the real "you". Hold still while I trim your moustache.'

'Hey, don't you touch my 'tache!'

'Too late. I've done one side already. Now you'll have to let me do the other or it'll be lopsided.'

Talker groaned and closed his eyes rather than watch his precious whiskers falling to the floor.

'There!' Aunt Cis stood back to admire her handiwork. 'My word, you look like a new man already. Sprog, did you find anything respectable in the bag of clothes I'd collected for the jumble?'

'How about this?' He held up a grey pin-stripe suit that had once belonged to Mr Pritchard the newsagent. 'I reckon it'll look okay, especially if he wears it with this white shirt and red bow tie.'

'A red bow tie? Well, I suppose it is Christmas Day.' Aunt Cis took the clothes from Sprog and handed them over to Talker. 'Here, take these into the front room and change.'

Grumbling, Talker disappeared.

When he reappeared ten minutes later they both stared at him in amazement.

'He certainly looks different,' said Aunt Cis. 'The question is, does he look like a vet?'

Sprog regarded the old man with a critical eye. A pity the suit wasn't a better fit: Talker was so skinny, about half the size of Mr Pritchard. And the bow tie was a bit skew-whiff. Even so, it was a remarkable transformation. Surely no one would recognize the small man with a neat white moustache and short-back-and-sides haircut as Talker Harris?

'It'll do,' Sprog said. 'After all, he's not supposed to be the proper vet, only a substitute. Come on, Talker. Let's go.'

'Wait! He needs one more thing . . .' Aunt Cis emptied her capacious handbag and gave it to Talker. 'This should make him look as if he means business.'

'Here, I'm not carrying no lady's handbag!' protested Talker.

'That's your *medical* bag,' Aunt Cis informed him. 'Every vet has one. Now goodbye – and good luck!'

When the doorbell rang Charley rushed to answer it, but found that her mother had already opened the door.

'The vet?' Mrs Spruce stared at the strange old man on the doorstep. 'But we don't need a vet. You must be mistaken.'

'No, he isn't.' Charley pushed forward and seized Talker by the hand. 'Come on, this way.' She dragged him along the hall to the study.

'Charlotte, you mustn't go in there,' pleaded Mrs Spruce. 'Can't you see your father's put up the DO NOT DISTURB sign?'

Charley pretended she hadn't heard. She pushed Talker into the room and closed the door firmly behind them before her mother could follow. 'Here he is,' she announced. 'I brought the vet.'

'At last!' Mr Spruce was too preoccupied to look up. 'I thought you'd never come. Do something, quick!'

Talker stood by the door, gripping his bag and staring at the scene in front of him. Mr Spruce, weak with exhaustion, his clothes in disarray, lay amidst the wreckage of his once-tidy study, holding grimly on to Achilles, who seemed not at all exhausted. The little dinosaur's body writhed and twisted as he fought to free himself, his tail switched from side to side, and he made a high bleating noise of great distress.

'Get a move on, man,' urged Mr Spruce. 'Give it something to calm it down.'

But Talker didn't move. He might have been turned to stone.

'Oh, I daresay it's come as a bit of a shock. Fact is, I was going to call you anyway to be a witness. But we'll talk about that in a minute. Right now I want you to give it a shot. Knock it unconscious, that's all I ask.'

Talker's mouth opened and shut without a sound coming out. Charley gave him a push forward.

'For heaven's sake, I'd do it myself if I had my instruments handy. A quick jab is all it will take.' Mr Spruce stopped as he caught sight of Talker. 'You're not George Hogben,' he said accusingly.

'No,' said Talker in a gruff, strained voice.

'No, I ain't. I'm a – a substitute.'

'Well, I don't care who you are as long as you come here and give me a hand.'

Talker took a step backwards. 'I'm not touching no dragon!'

'It's all right, it won't hurt you. Can't you see it's only a baby – ow!' He let out a yell as Achilles lashed his tail, catching him across the chest.

'Oh, look!' Charley caught sight of a face at the window. 'There's Sprog.'

'Who? What?' Mr Spruce made an effort to turn round.

'I think he's trying to tell us something.' Charley went over to the window and opened it. 'Hello, Sprog. The vet's come, but he's a funny sort of man. He's afraid of the duckodile.'

Sprog peered past her. 'Hurry up, Talker!' he urged. 'Just grab Achilles and give him to me.'

Talker said nervously, 'That thing's wild as a ferret.'

'He won't be, I promise. I'll tell him to let you pick him up. Go on, Talker – now!'

Warily Talker approached Mr Spruce and his desperately wriggling captive. He put out a hand towards Achilles, but as soon as he touched the scaly skin he hastily snatched it back. 'No, I can't,' he wailed. 'It ain't natural . . .'

'Oh, for heaven's sake!' Charley said impatiently. 'Here, let me do it.'

Her father looked up in surprise, and when she tried to take Achilles away from him he held on even tighter. 'Charlotte, what are you doing? Don't be such a silly little – Oh!'

He gave a shout as Achilles finally managed to break free and leapt into Charley's arms. She staggered back, almost losing her balance, and found herself close to the window.

'Quick, give him to me.' Sprog leaned over the sill and held out his hands.

Charley hesitated. Now that she was actually holding the duckodile she felt reluctant to let him go. After all, he was supposed to be her present.

'Charlotte!' Mr Spruce struggled to his feet. 'Don't you dare!'

But already the little creature had reached out both its short front arms and put them around Sprog's neck. 'Good boy,' Sprog murmured soothingly, lifting him over the sill. 'You're safe now. Good boy.'

'He seems to know you,' Charley said, a little sadly. 'I think he must be yours after all.'

'Thanks, Charley.' He looked past her into the room. 'Quick, Talker! Make a run for it.'

Talker already had his hand on the door handle. He wrenched it open and fled before Mr Spruce could stop him.

'You'd better go too,' Charley said.

'Yes, I had. 'Bye, Charley. You've been a real friend.'

She leaned over the window-sill to watch him racing down the path with his duckodile tucked under his arm. *A real friend*, he had called her! ''Bye, Sprog,' she shouted after him. 'Happy Christmas.'

Triumphantly Sprog charged through the back door of Dolphin Cottage. 'I've got him!' he yelled. 'I've got him back . . .'

He stopped dead. Aunt Cis wasn't alone. There was a tall man standing beside her and for one brief moment Sprog didn't recognize him. But then he did.

'Dad!' he exclaimed.

Chapter Sixteen

Good Boy

'So the minute the strike was over we jumped on the first plane home,' Dad explained as they sat round the kitchen table. 'And when we got to London we hired a car and drove straight here. Your mother was determined to be with you on Christmas Day.'

'Then where is she now?' Sprog asked, still bewildered by the speed at which things were happening. 'And Francis and Meg?'

But before Dad had time to answer the back door flew open and Talker burst in.

'Ah!' said Aunt Cis. 'We were wondering where you'd got to.'

'Did you get away okay?' asked Sprog. 'Mr Spruce didn't follow you here?'

Talker shook his head, too breathless to speak.

'You'd better sit down.' Aunt Cis pulled out a chair for him. 'Talker, this is my nephew, Peter Ogden. Sprog's father. Peter, this is Talker Harris.'

'Are you sure?' Dad stared at the strange old man wearing a suit several sizes too big for him and a crooked bow tie. 'He doesn't look at all the way Sprog described him.'

'No . . . well, there's a reason for that,' said Aunt Cis. 'But it's rather a long story.' She looked at Sprog.

'The fact is, Dad,' he said, 'Achilles is Minerva's son.'

Dad glanced curiously at the exhausted little creature curled up in his basket. 'You mean that's a − a −' He seemed reluctant to say the word.

'Another flaming dragon,' muttered Talker, who had by now got his breath back. 'And a whole load of trouble, just like the last one.'

'He's a corythosaurus,' Sprog told his father. 'Oh, I know you thought I was making it all up when I told you about Minerva. You only pretended to believe me, didn't you?'

Dad looked uncomfortable. 'Your mother said it was because you were away from home. She thought Minerva was your imaginary friend.'

Achilles stirred in his basket. 'Mama,' he murmured, even though he was asleep.

'I'm afraid that as long as he stays in this house he's in danger,' said Aunt Cis. 'Any minute now Mr Spruce will be round here, trying to get him back.'

Talker snorted. 'Not for a while, he won't! His wife just hit him over the head with a saucepan.'

'Why did she do that?' Sprog asked, amazed.

'To stop him rampaging around,' said Talker. 'She told her kids he was ill and they had to catch him. So off they went, and when they'd caught him she come up from behind and walloped him over the head with the pan.' He chuckled at the memory. 'She closed her eyes when she did it. Said she was sorry but it was for his own good.'

'How do you know all this?' asked Aunt Cis.

'I was hiding in the bushes, wasn't I? Took cover when old man Spruce came after me.' Talker was beginning to enjoy himself: there was nothing he liked better than a good audience. 'They sent the youngest one off to fetch

the doctor. That's when I made me getaway.'

Dad shook his head wonderingly. 'And I always thought this was such a quiet part of the world.'

Sprog said impatiently, 'Dad, you didn't answer my question. Where's Mum now – and Francis and Meg?'

'Waiting outside in the car. Francis and Meg are asleep, worn out after the long flight, and we didn't want to disturb them. Besides, it didn't seem fair for the entire family to descend on Aunt Cis without warning.'

'There's a turkey in the oven,' said Aunt Cis, 'and a pudding steaming on the hob. Four extra will be no trouble at all, if you care to go and fetch them.'

'That's very kind,' said Dad, smiling at his great aunt. 'And then we ought to be on our way. It's going to be a long drive to Aberdeen.'

'Aberdeen?' Sprog stared at him. 'You mean – we're going to Scotland?'

'Yes, of course. That's where I'll be working from now on, for North Sea oil. You'll love it there, Sprog. It's beautiful countryside.'

'I know. I've been there before.' He exchanged a look with Aunt Cis and guessed that, like him, she was thinking of their last visit to Scotland, when they had taken Minerva up to Loch Ness . . .

'Mama!' Achilles raised his head, suddenly wide awake. He started to clamber out of the basket. 'Mama, Mama!'

Sprog picked him up and held him close. 'Sssh, there's a good boy,' he said in thought language. But he knew now that Aunt Cis was right, he would never be able to keep Achilles as a pet. The danger was too great. And there was only one place where they could be sure he'd be safe and happy and well-looked-after.

'Don't worry,' he told Achilles, heavy-hearted. 'We'll take you to your mama.'

The shores of Loch Ness were deserted, the water looked grey and uninviting. Behind the loch rose the mountains, dark against the evening sky. Patched with snow, the country-side seemed much wilder and fiercer than the last time Sprog had come here, with Aunt Cis. But then, of course, it had been spring. Now it was the middle of winter.

'Minerva!' Sprog called with his mind.

The waters remained still, not a ripple broke the surface.

He shivered. 'Suppose she isn't there?'

'We'll wait,' said Mum. 'No hurry.'

Only she stood beside him on the shore. The rest of the family had stayed in the car, parked some distance away. Too many people might put Minerva off, he had warned them. Like her auntie, whom some called the Loch Ness monster, Minerva had good reason to be wary of humans. But he was glad Mum had come with him. Seeing her again had made him understand how Achilles felt; and even though Sprog would have taken great care of him the little dinosaur might have been lonely, especially as he grew older. Far better for him to be with his mother.

'Minerva!' he called again.

No movement in the loch.

He sighed and drew the blanket tighter around the sleeping Achilles. The drive had been long and tiring, even though the roads were almost empty: most people seemed to have stayed indoors, no doubt recovering from too much food on Christmas Day. Like Achilles, Meg and Francis had slept nearly all the way, Meg clutching the doll he had given her for Christmas. But now, at last, they had arrived.

He scanned the surface of the loch with anxious eyes. It was almost dark now and the water looked so cold. And deep. And mysterious.

'Water?' Achilles raised his head from the blanket and blinked his eyes at the scene before them. 'Splash-splash?'

'In a minute,' Sprog said. 'In a minute you can splash.'

'Any luck?' Mum asked.

'Not yet. I'll try again.' This time he closed his eyes to make it easier to concentrate. 'Minerva! Minerva!'

'Mama!' called Achilles. 'Mama, mama!'

'Look!' breathed Mum. 'Sprog, look – over there . . .'

He opened his eyes and looked. Something dark had appeared above the surface, a head that was strangely familiar . . . a long neck, followed by a large body . . . and it was swimming towards them, sending ripples across the loch.

'Is it her?' Mum whispered.

'I – I think so.' His throat had gone dry and croaky.

Suddenly, taking him by surprise, Achilles

wriggled out of his arms and plopped on to the shingle. 'Mama, mama!' he cried, and before Sprog could stop him he had plunged fearlessly into the water.

'Achilles, come back!' Sprog started down the bank, but his mother grabbed his arm.

'No, let him go,' she said. 'He'll be all right. Look, he's swimming towards her.'

'He's only little,' Sprog said. 'What if he drowns?'

'She won't let him drown.'

Unconvinced, Sprog watched Achilles until he was no more than a small dot. There were two larger shapes in the water now. Had Minerva's auntie come to join them? He watched as all three shapes, two large and one small, met together. They merged . . . and splashed . . . and finally dived.

And then the water was still again.

'There, what did I tell you? He'll be happy now. They both will.' Mum was still holding on to his arm. 'Come on, let's go back to the car.'

But he couldn't bear to leave, not without making sure. 'You go back. I want to stay a minute longer.'

'Well, as long as it's only a minute.'

Left alone, he kept his eyes fixed on the

water. 'Oh, Minerva,' he called. 'Is he all right? Please tell me if he's all right.'

The waters parted and a skinny arm waved to him from the centre of the loch. 'Thank you, Sprog. Thank you . . .'

'Minerva?' He could only just hear her, she was so far away. 'Is that really you?'

'I knew you'd bring . . . my little egg . . .'

'His name's Achilles . . .'

'Nice name . . . I like it.' And then she said something else he couldn't quite catch. Was it 'goodbye'? No, that wasn't right. It sounded more like 'Good boy'. Yes, that was it! *Good boy.*

Satisfied, Sprog turned and went to join his waiting family.

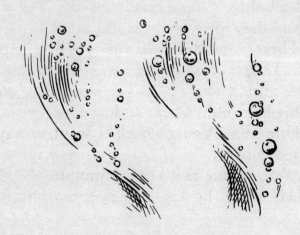